Eutopia

The Gnostic Land of
Prester John
A Novella

First published by O Books, 2010
O Books is an imprint of John Hunt Publishing Ltd., The Bothy, Deershot Lodge, Park Lane, Ropley,
Hants, SO24 0BE, UK
office1@o-books.net
www.o-books.net

Distribution in:	South Africa
	Stephan Phillips (pty) Ltd
UK and Europe	Email: orders@stephanphillips.com
Orca Book Services	Tel: 27 21 4489839 Telefax: 27 21 4479879
orders@orcabookservices.co.uk	
Tel: 01202 665432 Fax: 01202 666219	Text copyright Alan Jacobs 2008
Int. code (44)	
	Design: Stuart Davies
USA and Canada	
NBN	ISBN: 978 1 84694 275 4
custserv@nbnbooks.com	
Tel: 1 800 462 6420 Fax: 1 800 338 4550	All rights reserved. Except for brief quotations
	in critical articles or reviews, no part of this
Australia and New Zealand	book may be reproduced in any manner without
Brumby Books	prior written permission from the publishers.
sales@brumbybooks.com.au	
Tel: 61 3 9761 5535 Fax: 61 3 9761 7095	The rights of Alan Jacobs as author have been
	asserted in accordance with the Copyright,
Far East (offices in Singapore, Thailand,	Designs and Patents Act 1988.
Hong Kong, Taiwan)	
Pansing Distribution Pte Ltd	
kemal@pansing.com	A CIP catalogue record for this book is available
Tel: 65 6319 9939 Fax: 65 6462 5761	from the British Library.

Printed by Digital Book Print

Eutopia

The Gnostic Land of
Prester John
A Novella

Alan Jacobs

BOOKS

Winchester, UK
Washington, USA

CONTENTS

Dedicated to my late wife Claire
My dear companion on the quest.

Chapter 1

Arrival

From the mountains on every side, rivulets descended that filled all the valley with verdure and fertility, and formed a lake in the middle inhabited by fish of every species, and frequented by every fowl whom nature has taught to dip the wing in water. This lake discharged its superfluities by a stream which entered a dark cleft of the mountain on the northern side, and fell with dreadful noise from precipice to precipice till it was heard no more.
    Dr Samuel Johnson, from *Rasselas*, chapter 1

The magnificent, the beautiful, the most gracious Queen of Sheba, the refined, noble Prince Rasselas of Abyssinia, the great Magi, Emperor Prester John of Christendom, King Solomon the Wise of ancient Israel – all these high names had reverberated through my bodily frame since boyhood, when I had first become enchanted by Dr Samuel Johnson's fine and only novel *Rasselas*.

I had often wondered if that legend of the miraculous Happy Valley he vividly portrayed had ever existed. Such a possibility had excited many explorers, past and present. I decided to research the question in some depth. This eventually led me to search for Amhara, the land of the 'Happy Valley', the lost kingdom of Prince Rasselas.

This fascination determined that I must explore Ethiopia to see what I could find. When I left for Addis Ababa, somehow all these magic names resonated with the leonine roar of the Ethiopian Airways jet, thundering along the flight path as I braced myself to descend eventually like a golden eagle into magical Ethiopia, fresh from the tarmac at Heathrow.

As we soared above the clouds in brilliant sunshine, I mused on the Queen of Sheba, dark and swarthy, renowned as the most beautiful woman the world has ever known, whose delicate footsteps ever trod our Mother Earth. She was as sleek and graceful as an Abyssinian gazelle shining on a moonlit night. Her beryl eyes gleamed like the morning star.

But enough of this fantasy. First let me tell you who I am. My name is Justin, Justin Hart. I am an explorer. I am impelled by some strong kind of inner daemon to tell you about the greatest adventure of my life. It led me to rediscover the almost impossible, the ancient Gnostic, legendary land of Prester John, Amhara. I call my memoirs of the most astounding discovery I have ever made since I became an explorer 'Eutopia'. Why do I call it Eutopia? Well it turned out that Amhara was a Utopia and I was absolutely eu phoric when I discovered it. Also I recalled from my school days that the Greek eu meant good or well, and in this Eutopia everything was very good and very well! But enough of that for the moment, I will tell you all about Eutopia in due course, first I must tell you what made me start on this bizarre exploration. Eureka!

Amhara! What a mystic-sounding name. Mythologically Amhara was reputed to be the center of Emperor Prester John's vast ancient empire. It had been the home of my beloved Queen of Sheba.

These old legends have intrigued me ever since I first read about the Happy Valley, the earthly paradise so eloquently described by Sam Johnson. Ethiopia is the only remaining region in mysterious Africa that has maintained its original character since earliest antiquity. I had long hoped to explore this mysterious land. What was more, I would be following in the footsteps of great Victorian explorers like Sir Richard Burton and the illustrious French poet, Arthur Rimbaud. Now that we were gently cruising above the clouds my thoughts mused on the Happy

Valley. This was an earthly utopia where the ancient Abyssinian princes and princesses were mercifully confined, to be protected, uncontaminated by the many evils of the tumultuous world outside. The valley was lavishly provided with all the possible means of happiness that this planet could provide. It was surrounded by snow-capped mountains reflecting the changing sunlight from scarlet dawn to golden dusk. The valley was irrigated by clear blue streams and the whole plateau was rich with emerald green, velvet vegetation, bursting with rampant fertility. A vast, still sapphire lake in the center was inhabited by every species of fish and water fowl imaginable.

The buxom mountainsides were covered with every known variety of deciduous and evergreen tree and the banks of the brooks were flanked by exotically colorful flowers, red, yellow, orange, purple, pink and blue. Many varied fruit orchards and fields of vegetables and cereal crops grew in rich and plentiful abundance. All varieties of wild animals wandered about in the shrub lands, while flocks of sheep and cattle grazed on the lush green pastures. The land was peopled by a tall handsome black race of incredible nobility.

It would indeed be truly wonderful if by some miracle I could stumble upon the Happy Valley, which up to now had escaped all the searches of ancient and modern explorers. Even James Bruce, the indefatigable Scottish adventurer on whose travels Dr. Johnson based his novel, never actually found the Happy Valley, although he visited Ethiopia to search for it. Since ancient times the Happy Valley was believed to be in the region where the great empire of the legendary Prester John was centered.

What, I pondered, would I discover in the Happy Valley if ever I found it? I was determined when we arrived at Addis to carefully prepare plans for an expedition. If the fates were kind to me I would land up in this earthly paradise. Deep down I had a sneaking suspicion that there was a good chance this would happen, irrational though it may be. I dozed off, dreaming of

Prince Rasselas, the fourth son of the mighty emperor of Abyssinia, descended from the great King Menelik, the handsome lovechild of wise King Solomon and the beautiful Queen of Sheba.

Prince Rasselas' philosopher-tutor, the sage Imlac, only increased Rasselas' desire to visit the outside world, like Prince Siddhartha, the Buddha, to see for himself the suffering humanity supposed to live outside the palace gates. Rasselas eventually escaped into the dense world of Egypt with his sister and a maidservant. Their observations led them to conclude that "Human life is everywhere in a state in which much is to be endured and little to be enjoyed". Many adventures followed, and their pretty maidservant was abducted for a sheikh's harem. Eventually Rasselas concluded that real happiness in the outside world was really illusory and the search for it there was futile.

"Our hopes cannot be fulfilled in this world of transience," said Rasselas. Yet here was I planning to find their Happy Valley, quixotic fool that I am. I was awakened from my reverie by the stewardess informing us over the address system that we would shortly be landing at Addis Ababa and please to fasten our seat belts.

Chapter 2

Addis Ababa

Nor where Abassin Kings their issue guard,
Mount Amara, though this by some supposed
True Paradise, under the Ethiop line
By Nilus heads, enclosed with shining rock,
A whole day's journey high.
John Milton, from *Paradise Lost*, Book IV, 280

The name *Addis Ababa* means 'new flower'. It serves as the capital and commercial center of Ethiopia. Now a teeming city of nearly four million, it was founded by another, much later, Emperor, named Menelik, the first modernizer of Ethiopia in the latter part of the 19th century.

A large, sprawling, hospitable city, Addis nestles in the foothills of Mount Enoto. Modern-style buildings nudge each other side by side with medieval historic churches, palaces and royal monuments. A vast forest of country-style huts seems to extend forever, giving it an unmistakable air of an African village jostling with a modern European city. I could smell the warm air filled with the intoxicating fragrance of flowers and eucalyptus trees.

I felt, in a strange and haunting way, that I was about to come home. After the routine clearing of customs, I collected my backpacker's rucksack and was greeted by a rotund friendly Ethiopian who spoke tolerable English. "Come with me, sir, and I will lead you to my great-uncle's taxi. He will make you a very good price and take you to a good hotel. Come."

As it was my usual habit to accept gratefully most things that life offered, I followed him to a rather battered black cab. He introduced me to his great-uncle, who surprisingly looked about the same age, and my baggage was bundled into the boot. Belching poisonous fumes from the exhaust we accelerated sharply and started the 8km drive from the airport to the center of the city.

I had fleeting glimpses of well-built men and women in white robes and colorful turbans or burkas, red, green, blue, and yellow, lounging outside their huts. As we approached the town I began to feel at home, noticing familiar names such as Eden Street, Churchill Street and George VI Avenue. Horse-drawn gharries and scooter rickshaws raced in between pedestrians and battered old jalopies along the wide boulevards.

The men and women mainly wore white cloaks, but a colorful array of the many different-colored sashes, shawls and headgear gave a festive feeling to the scene, as if it was some great carnival. There was a sprinkling of western-dressed businessmen and bureaucrats in tailored lounge suits and workers wearing the ubiquitous, almost universal blue jeans and T-shirts, with the odd baseball cap, looking somewhat out of place.

The taxi pulled up rather sharply at a hotel signposted the Casa Populaire. It reminded me of a university college quadrangle, shaped with what could have been a cloister in the center. The four-square building was divided by staircases, with suites on each floor. After being handed over to the receptionist by my driver and tipping him generously, I was allocated a room on the top floor. A youthful bellboy lifted my baggage on his back and led me up the rough concrete staircase.

The room was spartan, but clean. There was an iron bedstead, a cotton mattress, a generous wardrobe, a simple chair and a small table. It adjoined a bathroom with, thank goodness, a western-style toilet, a cast-iron bath and a hand basin.

My ruminations on how to proceed with the expedition led me to the inevitable conclusion that I was helpless on my own. I needed the companionship of an intelligent, educated, strong Ethiopian who could be my guide, and together we could make the necessary logistical decisions.

By now I was very hungry. I consulted my East African guidebook and was attracted by the sound of the Karamara Restaurant on Africa Avenue, where they offered entertainment by strolling troubadours and musicians, with an authentic Ethiopian cuisine.

As I strolled in the direction of Revolution Square and Obole Road where the Karamara was located, I was amazed at the variety of interesting buildings confronting me. They seemed a unique and exotic blend of African and late-European colonial styles, with their own unplanned enchantment. After admiring the huge natural amphitheater in Revolution Square I spotted the Karamara.

I was greeted by the lively sound of drumbeats accompanying African chant. These ululations always sent a primeval thrill tingling through my limbs. I sat down at a vacant table and my eyes were caught by a fine-looking, middle-aged Ethiopian who knowingly stared at me with a concentrated, uncanny gaze. It was as if we had known each other somewhere before and he was waiting for me. It was as if I had always known this soul, staring out at me behind his big brown eyes, yet he was totally unknown to me as a person. There was some instant recognition that the strong hand of destiny was taking hold of me against any instincts I might have to the contrary.

He had refined features, speaking of some education and culture. I could not resist an impulse – a strange thing for me to do, against my natural British reserve. Here I am in Ethiopia for the first time ever, and I badly need some travel advice.

"I hope you might be so kind as to assist me?" I hesitatingly asked.

"Yes, of course." It seemed as natural a thing as daylight.

"Come, sit yourself down at my table and we'll eat together,"

I said.

"What is it you wish to know, my friend?" He moved and joined me at my table, sitting opposite me. We both looked at each other with a certain 'knowingness', which was very strange. A strong sense of deja vu was overwhelming me, leaving me silent for some minutes.

After a respectful pause he introduced himself. "I am Tafara. And you are...?"

"My name is Justin, Justin Hart, to be precise." He held out his palm and we shook hands firmly. "Look," I said. "There's no point in beating about the bush: I am here on a mission, and I need some advice."

"I shall listen patiently, my friend. Let's talk while we eat together." He ordered us some *wot*, a hot spicy stew of vegetables seasoned with *berbere*. It was served with *injera*, a spongy, bread pancake made from fermented flour batter. It was a good way of mopping up the juices from the wot. He also sent for some *gondar*, a local red wine. Fortunately the music had stopped for the time being, so I could begin my story.

"I'm coming straight to the point," I said, somewhat abruptly. "I'm going to look for the Happy Valley."

"What?" He looked at me as if he had made some kind of mistake, talking to an eccentric Englishman, a bit off-the-wall, not a soul-brother after all.

"Yes," I said, gaining confidence. "The Happy Valley of Prince Rasselas, the Queen of Sheba and Emperor Prester John." It was as if a sip of the strong wine had gone to my head, the way I blurted everything out.

"Ah!" His face changed from querulous, broadening into a warm, beaming smile. "I know, you have come to search, like many others, for Amhara!"

I was amazed at the synchronicity and serendipity of all that had happened. "How on earth did you know that?" I replied.

"Oh, I read most of the literature when I was at university, to learn how Westerners regard our country. You are all fascinated by our legends."

He fell into silence for a moment, and then said: "I think I know the general direction in which to head, but we will have to hire mules and buy supplies."

"Where do we head for, then?" I asked, hardly concealing my surprise and delight.

"The area we will need to search is approximately 250 miles north of here. Somewhere in a square south of the Simian Mountains. Gondar – that is their wine you are drinking – in the north, and Dessie in the south, with Waldia in the west and Lake Tana in the east."

"How could you possibly know all this?"

"Well, I studied it at the university here. We know historically that the Abyssinian emperors confined their princes and princesses in Ambars, in the isolated mountains of this region, to insulate them from the violent world outside. This inspired your Scottish explorer Bruce to write about it in his travel books, and Dr Samuel Johnson romanticized it in his novel *Rasselas*. He took it from Bruce, I suppose."

I was stunned by his erudition, and was quietly full of mounting joy at his responses. Then the music started, drowning conversation for a while. There were chanting to a haunting melody, rapid drumming and screaming ululations, beloved of local women. We decided to finish our wine and enjoy the show. Tafara said he would visit me at my hotel tomorrow, about ten in the morning, to discuss preparations for a joint expedition.

Chapter 3

Tafara

1. And when the Queen of Sheba heard the fame of Solomon concerning the name of the Lord, she came to prove him with hard questions.
2. And she came to Jerusalem with a very great train, with camels that bore spices, and very much gold, and precious stones: and when she was come to Solomon, she communed with him of all that was in her heart.
13. And King Solomon gave unto the Queen of Sheba all her desire, whatsoever she asked, beside that which Solomon gave her of his royal bounty. So she turned and went to her own country, she and her servants.
The *Book of Kings*, chapter 10

Tafara arrived promptly at the Casa Populaire and we sat either side of my table. I ordered some of that superb Ethiopian coffee from the bellboy and we sat down. He had brought some maps, which he unrolled.

"Well", he began, "I suggest, to save time, we hire a Jeep and I'll drive it up to Dessie. From there we must hire mules as all the roads are not suitable for mountain exploration, and the Jeep wouldn't make the crags. Then we drive across the Wollo to Bethlehem – we have a town with the same name as Jesus' birth-place – and then we skirt Mount Garen to get to Debra Tabor at Enfraz."

He traced the journey on the map while he was talking. "Then we pass Addis Zemen and we enter the area where your so called Happy Valley could be hidden, near Mount Wehni."

"Look," I said, curbing his enthusiasm. "This is very impressive, but what makes you think that the Happy Valley, if it exists at all, might be near Mount Wehni?"

"Well, in these highlands there are a wealth of mountains called Ambars. They are flat-topped and sheer sided. In medieval times, say around the 10th Century, it was decided to house all the male heirs to the throne on an Ambar called Debra Damo. This confinement was designed to prevent any revolutions or plotting against the monarchy – such were those days.

"The custom died out at the end of the 10th Century, but it was revived in the 13th. Then an Amba called Geshen was chosen for the royal mountain prison. This was the main source for Sam Johnson's *Rasselas*, which he worked out from travelers' accounts of Amba Geshen. In actual fact, by the 18th century when Johnson wrote his book, Geshen had been replaced by Wachni."

All this time Tafara had been tracing the map with his forefinger, pointing out the places he mentioned. I was astonished and most impressed at his knowledge. He continued his narrative.

"It was not until twenty years after Rasselas that the famous traveler and explorer, James Bruce of Kinnaird, finally returned to England after spending two whole years at the royal court in Gondar. He told many stories about Wachni. His book, which I read at the university, was called *Travels to Discover the Source of the Nile*, and it caused a sensation in your country at the time. It is in six volumes, we have a complete copy in the library where I studied."

I nodded as if to say yes, although most of what he was saying was new to me. I had heard about Bruce, but that was about all.

He went on: "As far as I can make out, since then only one other European traveler has actually visited the site. Your infamous Sir Richard Burton and the crazy French poet Rimbaud were too busy searching in other directions, like Harrar. There, where we are talking about, it is a wilderness.

"But the young Tom Pakenham, a son of your recently-deceased saintly Lord Longford, did reach the mountain in the 1950s. He never found the Amhara you are looking for, but he did explore the area where it may have been, according to hints that he picked up from the locals. But he gave up eventually."

"Oh!" I exclaimed in astonishment. Pakenham was not a name I had come across either. "But please go on."

"Well, Wheni was the main royal prison, and that is where we shall be heading." It sounded as if he had assumed I would employ him. "We'll scour the area all around it. Well, there it is then, Wheni." He became more and more emphatic, and I was feeling somewhat impressed by his knowledge and presence.

He continued, "So we go to Enfraz and follow Pakenham's route to the Belesa Mountains. Did you know he wrote a travel book called *The Mountains of Rasselas*?"

"No," I said, exposing my ignorance once again. "I know what, let's have some more coffee." I called the waiter and ordered more coffee. I discovered this coffee drinking could be quite a ritual in this country. The pure Abyssinian coffee is served somewhat like in Turkey, in small copper cups, sipped very slowly and seriously.

"Did you know that we discovered coffee for the whole world?" said Tafara while we were drinking.

"No."

"I'll tell you, then. There was once a goat-herder called Kaldi who lived in the highlands where we are going, around the year 300 after Christ. One day his goats became extremely frisky after feeding on the berries of a certain bush. Even the very oldest goats started to dance about, so Kaldi became very curious to find out about the properties of this bush. He took some of the red berries to a nearby monastery, where the monks were knowledgeable on all kinds of local matters.

"The monks experimented by throwing the beans inside the berries into boiling water. They produced a pleasant smelling brew and it tasted very good, if somewhat bitter. It definitely enlivened the monks, and from then on they used to drink some before midnight mass, in order to keep awake. So, see what we Ethiopians have given to humanity! Where would your modern man be without his cup of coffee?"

I replied, "I had always suspected there was something special about coffee. I remember Gurdjieff saying, when I studied his teachings…"

At the mention of the name Gurdjieff his eyes narrowed and he gazed at me in a concentrated way. I let this pass for a moment, but instinctively I could sense that there was something very special if this fine Ethiopian knew something about the charismatic mystic Gurdjieff, and perhaps about mysticism in general – much more perhaps than he was giving away.

I continued. "Yes, George Gurdjieff said that the coffee in Europe was not of the same quality as in the Middle East, and that the Sufis used it as a drink to bring them closer to God. I think he said that, like tea, tobacco and other substances, it contained a complete enneagram. That is to say the Laws of Seven and Three were combined."

He interrupted, "Yes, the word 'coffee' is derived from our word for wine, and we have had Sufis here. The Aidarusiyya Taiba of Tarim spread down the East African coast, so who knows what they discovered?

"Yes," I said, "Gurdjieff was truly a remarkable man".

"Yes, I know," he replied. "I have read his books".

"Well," I said. "You're hired! How much do you want me to pay you for being my guide?"

He laughed. "Oh, just meet the expenses. I will enjoy being with you and sharing the adventure. But if we find Amhara, then promise you'll give me half of any treasure we may come across."

"Okay!" I said. "The deal is done!"

Having finished our coffee we agreed to meet the next day to drive to Dessie in a Jeep. But first I said that I wanted to congratulate him on his knowledge about what I was looking for.

"I will let you into a little secret", he said with a twinkle in his eye. "When I was very young, I served as a carrier in Tom Pakenham's expedition. He was a very fine man, rather young at the time, fresh from university, but very daring."

Again I was stunned. What is more, I again felt, very forcibly, that the iron hand of destiny had taken over this whole adventure and delivered me into the hands of this Tafara, who had already traveled to these parts. What more could I wish for?

"Tell me," I asked, "before you leave, what do you know about Prester John?"

"Ah! One of the greatest men who ever trod our Mother Earth, but now largely forgotten in the West. He was one of those rare beings, an emperor and at the same time a sage, a platonic philosopher-king. Because he was so hidden and secretive, his fame lies more in legend than in history. I believe that where we are heading may well be his heartland. Who knows what we may stumble on when we get there?" He laughed.

"And the Queen of Sheba?" I asked.

"Ah! There was a real woman for you! She was probably the most beautiful and wise woman the world has ever seen, and King Solomon's queen into the bargain! He is supposed to have taught her all his great wisdom".

"Another sage-king?" I asked.

"Obviously!" he replied.

"Now, what about the Ark of the Covenant?" I asked, hungry for more information from my new guide. "No, that's at Axum, near where we are going. It is a long story, but it was brought here by one of their love-sons, Menelik, before the destruction of the Temple in Jerusalem, for safekeeping. It turned us into a holy nation!"

"Well, well, Tafara," I said. "You are indeed a jewel amongst men. Let's go and hire that Jeep so we can collect it in the morning."

We went off to the hire firm Tafara knew. My British driving license was accepted and Tafara said he was a good driver. It was quickly arranged. I invited Tafara for lunch. Tafara accepted and said that after the meal we would both need time to pack and rest. We went to a simple restaurant Tafara knew, called the *Wutma*. We ordered a native dish of peas and lentils with *tibs*, a crisply fried steak. We sat at a brightly-colored table called a *marob*, eating with our hands. Tafara ordered the local beer called *talla*. I found it somewhat light for my taste, but quite drinkable.

Over lunch I told him what I knew about the story of Prester John, to see if he would fill me in with further information. "Prester John," I said, "was also called Presbyter John, John the Priest, John the Elder or John, Son of God. He was the hero of numerous legends in the medieval world around the times of the Crusades, about the 12th Century. According to the early chronicles of Hugh de Gerbal and Otto of Freising, he was a wealthy and powerful priest-king and a lineal descendent of the same three Magian kings who first visited the baby Jesus."

"Yes," said Tafara, "the Magi are indeed our link. The Magi who visited Jesus at his birth were also descended from the Queen of Sheba and King Solomon. Their love-child Menelik was sent by Solomon to found a holy state in the area where we are heading. That's how the Ark of the Covenant found its way there. Now David, the second son of Solomon, was the ancestor of Jesus through the line of Jesse, so you see we have a perfect circle of influence through King Solomon, the Queen of Sheba, the Lord Jesus and the Emperor Prester John, all held together by the three wise kings of the Magi at the Nativity."

This was the kind of insight I hoped would come up, so I went on to ask Tafara to tell me about the Magi and who they were.

"Well, the Three Wise Men who visited the infant Jesus were the three kings, Melchior, Gaspar and Balthazar. The first offered gold, the emblem of royalty, the second frankincense, in token of divinity, and the third myrrh, a prophetic allusion to the persecution of Jesus, leading to his crucifixion as the man of sorrows. Melchior is Hebrew for 'King of Light', Gaspar derives from an old Persian word *kansbar*, meaning 'treasurer', and Balthazar comes from the Babylonian protector of the king.

"Among the ancient Medes and Persians, the Magi were a priestly caste with occult and magical powers. In Camoens' *The Lusiad* the term is synonymous with the Indian Brahmin Rishis. This is very significant, and Ammianus Marcellinus says the Zoroastrian Magi derived all their knowledge from the Rishis, the composers of the *Rig Veda* and the famed *Upanishads*. Their Vedic center in Harappa and Mohenjo-Daro, in the Indus valley, fertilized by migration all the great civilizations of the ancient world – Chaldea, Canaan, Persia, Greece, Egypt and of course King Solomon's kingdom of Israel, the cradle of Christianity and Islam."

"What about their magic?" I asked.

"Well, magic was the science of Abraham, Orpheus, Zoroaster and Moses. Their science was graven on tablets of stone by Enoch and Hermes Trismegistus, the father of the Western esoteric tradition. The Holy Kabbalah was revealed by Moses. The Eleusian and Theban mysteries derive from Hermes, as does the knowledge of the modern Rosicrucians and early Freemasons."

This indeed was a pyrotechnic display of esoteric knowledge. I knew now that there was plenty of questioning left for me to follow up in due course with Tafara.

"Now," said Tafara, "tell me more about what you know of our emperor Prester John".

"Well, as far as I can remember, about the mid-14th Century Ethiopia became the focus for the search to find the center of the legendary Christian empire of Prester John. It was a huge empire, wisely ruled, with many kings and dukes under the emperor's dominion. Its boundaries were vast and extended into southern Africa and western India. Nobody knows the exact limits. We will continue the conversation on our journey. Who knows what we might find when we get near Mount Wehni, possibly the hidden capital of Prester John's empire? Who knows?"

Chapter 4

The Journey to Dessie

We have hoisted the Standard of St George on the mountains of Rasselas.

Benjamin Disraeli, on the British expedition to Abyssinia, 1867-68

We hired a surplus US Army Jeep, which looked robust and roadworthy. I had packed my rucksack with sleeping bag, tent, pullover, warm jacket and waterproof coat. Tafara had brought similar. He had also packed some books, which somewhat surprised me.

He drove and we set off along the well-metalled road out of Addis, past the village huts and into the broad savannah. Tafara concentrated on the road and hardly spoke. We aimed to reach Dessie by the evening, so he stepped on it. I saw occasional herds of goats, cattle and groups of nomadic tribesmen. The landscape was hot and dusty, but as we motored north it became more hilly and I could see mountains on the horizon. The sky was a brilliant turquoise and I was pleased to spot both a green wood hoopoe and a tawny eagle.

That evening we reached Dessie, a fine old, mainly-Muslim town, situated picturesquely in a steep valley. We drove up to the Ambaras Hotel, which looked very clean and boasted hot showers and a restaurant.

"Tomorrow," said Tafara, "we hire the mules. Tonight we eat."

The Ambaras served us a spicy fish curry, one of the best I have ever eaten. We ordered the local Axiemite wine, which went down very well with some raisin cakes.

Tafara put one of his books on the table. "Justin, do you really know what we are actually looking for? I am going to read to you Sir John Mandeville's account of Prester John's kingdom. Admittedly it was based on hearsay."

I sipped my wine and listened to his deep resonant tones as he read from chapter 30 of Sir John's exhaustive book of travels.

"*This Emperor, Prester John, holds full great land and hath many full noble cities and good towns in his realm, and many great diverse isles, and large. For all the country of Ind...*" Here Tafara broke off and said "Mandeville wrote in the 14th Century and somehow grouped Abyssinia together as one country called 'Ind'."

Then he continued reading: "*Ind is devised in isles for the great floods that come from Paradise, that depart all the land in many parts. And also in the sea he hath full many isles. And the best city in the Isle of Pentexoire is Nyse, that is a full royal city and a noble, and full rich...* This book fuelled the mysterious legend of Prester John throughout the Middle Ages." Then he resumed reading.

"*This Prester John hath under him many kings and many isles and many diverse folk of diverse conditions, and this land is full good and rich, but not so rich as is the land of the great Chan...* Mandeville goes on to say that more people go to Chan and Cathay to buy goods because in the isle of Prester John there were great sea perils..."

Tafara laughed, and went on, "*For in many places of the sea be great rocks of stones of the adamant, that of his proper nature draweth iron to him. And therefore there pass no ships that have either bonds or nails of iron within them. And if there do, anon the rocks of the Adamants draw them to them, that never they may go thence. I myself have seen afar in that sea, as though it had been a great isle full of trees and buscaylle, full of thorns and briars, great plenty.*"

"What a curious, archaic style," I said.

"Yes," said Tafara. "Mandeville was hardly a literary stylist in the modern sense." He laughed again. "Funny ideas they had in those days." He continued reading, "*And the shipmen told us, that all that was of ships that were drawn thither by the Adamants, for the iron that was in them."*

"I'll skip a bit... But it does show that in some way Prester John's kingdom was always protected, a kind of hidden place, difficult to get to and find. *And the merchants pass by the kingdom of Persia, and go to a city that is called Hermes, for Hermes the Philosopher founded it.* I'm skipping irrelevant details and will read what is more interesting. Now...

"*In the land of Prester John be many diverse things and many precious stones, so great and so large, that men make of them vessels, as platters, dishes and cups.* We go on... *The Emperor Prester John is Christian, and a great part of his country also. But yet, they have not all the articles of our faith as we have. They believe well, in the Father, the Son and the Holy Ghost. And they be full devout and right true one to another...*

"*And he hath under him 72 provinces, and in every province is a king. And these kings have kings under them, and all be tributaries to Prester John, and he hath in his lordships many great marvels.*"

"You see," said Tafara, "we are beginning to see that Prester John must have been what Plato called a philosopher-king, and could well have educated others to rule in his dominions. I shall skip a bit and read on... *This emperor Prester John, when he goeth into battle against any other lord, he hath no banners borne before him; but he hath three crosses of gold, fine, great and high, full of precious stones, and every of these crosses be set in a chariot, full richly arrayed...*"

I interrupted, "Yes, this shows he was obviously a very devout Christian."

"Yes, obviously, and it says... *In his principal palace, that is so rich and noble that no man will know it by estimation, but he had seen it. And above the chief tower of the palace be two round pommels of gold, and in every inch of them be two great carbuncles that shine full bright upon the night. And the principal gates of the palace be of precious stone, that men call sardonyx, and the border and the bars be of ivory. And the windows of the halls and chambers be of crystal. And the tables whereon men eat, some be of emeralds, some of amethyst and some of gold, full of precious stones; and the pillars that bear up the tables be of the same precious stones...* and so it goes on.

"But this may amuse you. *And the form of his bed is of fine sapphires, bended with gold, for to make him sleep well and to refrain him from lechery; for he will not lie with his wives but four times in the year, after the four seasons, and that is only for to engender children.*"

"Well, well," I said. "Quite a man!"

"So what do you think, Justin?"

"Well, he obviously was a very great emperor who made a tremendous impact upon the medieval world. Once a man becomes a legend it is difficult to distinguish fact from fancy, and myth from history, but a great sun must have been there shining behind the clouds."

"Yes, I agree. So let us retire for the night, and tomorrow we shall start our journey."

Chapter 5

Bethlehem

All they from Sheba shall come; they shall bring gold and incense; and they shall shew forth the praises of the Lord.
    The *Book of Isaiah*, LX, v7

Early next morning after breakfast we drove the Jeep to the car-hire firm's Dessie office to return it, and we took their advice about mule hire. Mules were easy to rent, for many tourists came to trek in these highlands, to see the magnificent Blue Nile Falls, Lalibela with its ancient carved-rock churches, Debra, Gondar and the huge Lake Tana with its exotic wildlife. But we were heading for the mountainous Belesa region where Europeans rarely venture, where there are only scrublands and highlands.

We found two sturdy-looking beasts which we nicknamed Ham and Cush. I took Ham and Tafara rode Cush. We hoisted our packs and then went to the market to buy provisions. Tafara told me we needed enough food to reach Bethlehem, about two days' trek. I left the haggling to Tafara, who seemed very experienced in this kind of activity.

East Africa's highlands are like no other, and nowhere are the differences more sharply noticeable than in this giant wilderness over which Ham and Cush were steadfastly plodding along. Rugged peaks, some more than 4,000 meters high, with occasional glimpses of rolling emerald-green moorlands, laced with fissures. Hidden springs create occasional oases. The unique mountain wildlife, birds, flora and still, blue lakes add to the enchantment.

Tafara had brought his compass and we left the potholed

road. As far as I was now concerned, we were totally entering into the unknown. The mules were docile and trod in measured paces which hardly varied. I was discovering that riding mules was a sore and demanding experience, and at times I walked, but this was a necessary price to pay for what was becoming a very special experience.

That day we spotted a simian fox, a serval cat, a colobus monkey and, in the distance through field glasses, I spotted a lone leopard. There were choughs like you have in most mountainous regions, blue-winged geese and thick-billed ravens, the local scavengers. The simian fox, unique to Ethiopia, is a handsome tawny-red creature with a black bushy tail.

Tafara said, "We must be as wily as the fox, brave as the leopard and stubborn as our mules if we wish to reach Amhara." I accepted his word for it.

We passed some nomadic herdsmen driving their mountain goats. I noticed their women wore black burkas – they must be Muslims. It was not very hot because we were up high. It reminded me of a balmy summer's day back home in England, with a clear blue sky and the occasional wandering lonely cloud.

On the way, during easier-going stretches, I questioned Tafara about the Magi. As it was midday, Tafara said he would tell me more over lunch. We halted by a small lake, where the mules could munch some lush grass and be watered, while we tucked into our spicy *injera* sandwiches. I saw some fish in the lake and regretted we didn't bring a net. They looked like salmon trout.

"Now tell me about the Magi," I asked. "I expect when we find, or rather *if* we find, Amhara, it will be governed by them?"

"Probably," said Tafara in an offhanded way. I began to wonder who this man really was. He seemed a veritable font of encyclopedic esoteric knowledge and wisdom.

"Well, such were the doctrines of the great Magi that they were the possessors of a knowledge that gave them mastery of the occult powers of nature. Hence *magic*..." He spelled out the letters M, A, G and I, then added a C on the end.

When Tafara was in this vein he sounded and looked very authoritative. "Please go on," I said.

"The sum of these secrets might be termed a form of transcendental fireworks, for it was intimately related to a deep knowledge of fire. We know that the ancient Vedic Rishis played great attention to fire. They had a lesser god called Agni, rather like the Greek Prometheus, an intermediary between Heaven and Earth. He brought down fire from Heaven and placed it on Earth. They even found out about electricity, but magic is a science which to abuse is to lose. After Assyria this kind of magic dwindled and the Kali Yuga or Iron Age of Darkness began.

"But there was always a saving grace, hidden from the eyes of those who cannot see or the ears of those who cannot hear, as Jesus put it. Abraham was a great magician and brought the knowledge of his teacher Melchizedek with him. Moses found it in Egypt, where he was a prince. There it gained a grade of completion, so to speak. Hermes took it into ancient Greece, and now we find their teachings of unity of being. Unity is the harmony in all things. Nature is always acting harmoniously, towards perfect balance – the natural correspondence between the Creator and the created, so to speak."

"I suppose, if we find Amhara, it will be based on these principles?"

"You can be certain that, if Prester John synthesized all this ancient knowledge, it will be. But we shall see, as the blind man said. We had better move on, if we wish to reach Bethlehem by tomorrow evening."

After another afternoon's trekking, my backside was beginning to feel sore; we camped by a stream and the mules rested. We lit a fire and cooked a stew of lentils, vegetables and herbs. Tafara caught a salmon trout in the stream with his bare hands and this we enjoyed with the stew. After supper, under the stars, I asked him to tell me some more about these Magi.

"Well, Moses took the wisdom and magic of Egypt with him when he led the Hebrews out of slavery. He wished to establish a holy nation and accordingly set out its laws. From this cradle of Israel came Solomon and eventually Jesus and Christianity, and later, from this same source, came Islam and the Sufis.

"Solomon was a great magician. He passed on his wisdom to our Queen of Sheba, who brought it to Ethiopia. Solomon resolved the name of God, Jehovah, into 72 explicatory names. The art of employing those names was the Key of Solomon, the foundation of the mystic Kabbalah, with its Sephiroth, which some Hassidic Jews still practice today."

"Did the Queen of Sheba obtain her gold by alchemy?"

"There was no need. She obtained all the gold, silver and precious stones she needed from her own mines at Bene-Shangal and Walaga. The Amhara and Galla chiefs know all about it. I expect there are many more precious minerals left in these hills."

"How about James Bruce, who came to these parts in the 18th century? He must have been a remarkable man."

"Yes, I believe he was. All Bruce's reports on Ethiopia proved to be accurate in spite of the suspicion held in your country about his truthfulness. Dr. Johnson took his description of Amhara from Portuguese sources. He thought Bruce was exaggerating about his story of life at the court of Emperor Ras at Gondar. Bruce brought back the original *Book of Enoch*, which the West had lost. He mapped the source of the Blue Nile.

"As a Freemason he was interested in the wisdom of Solomon, from where the knowledge of the Knights Templar came, when they excavated around the ruins of Solomon's Temple in Jerusalem. He also looked for the missing Ark of the Covenant at Axum, where they found the Queen of Sheba's bath, of all things. The original *Book of Enoch*, still untampered with by theologians, proposed that paradise existed as a physical place hidden in these parts. Probably Amhara.

"Yes, your Bruce emerges as one in a long line of British

savants, like John Dee, Francis Bacon, Isaac Newton and William Blake, up to the mysticism of AE Waite and his Order of the Golden Dawn, which influenced your Irish poet WB Yeats. It is time Bruce received his due recognition in the great chain of esoteric knowledge which enlightens what otherwise would be one hell of a world."

It was time to settle down under the mantle of night, studded with the twinkling diamonds of the constellations. I dreamed happily about a great meeting in a golden canopy with King Solomon, the Queen of Sheba and a tall commanding figure with a Christ-like face, whom I took to be Prester John.

When I was awakened by the light of a fiery dawn, we break-fasted, then mounted Ham and Cush, ready for the trek to Abyssinian Bethlehem. I admired our indefatigable pack-mules and their surefootedness as we climbed the rocky slopes where no Jeep could ever reach. I recalled the words of the famous traveler Rosa Forbes who, at the beginning of the century, said that the crags were like great chess pieces created by the gods, in colors of emerald, gold and lapis lazuli.

After a steep descent down the rocky side of a gorge we splashed over a ford. We had now entered a different landscape, a featureless tundra steppe, unploughed and ungrazed. We climbed up the saddle of a long ridge. The whole country lay outstretched like a map at our feet. There were brown massifs, dizzy chasms and a spiky panorama of bluish peaks in the distance. Near us, the ridge suddenly dipped and unexpectedly revealed a series of watered emerald green valleys, dotted with villages and eucalyptus trees.

"Over there," said Tafara, "lies our Bethlehem."

By noon we had reached a high plateau. Then we descended through a beautiful juniper forest. Coming out of the woods, the path fell in rapid spirals to the village of Bethlehem, with its large circular church. I felt the magic inherent in this strange, almost impenetrable land – except to local inhabitants and the most intrepid travelers.

Bethlehem church had a façade covering a much older building inside. The original church was medieval and rectangular with pink stone walls, polished like porphyry. Frescoes had once been hung there, but only the marks were left. We sat in the churchyard under some fig trees and slaked our thirst with fresh spring water, drinking straight out of a gourd. Perhaps this little village called Bethlehem had some mysterious relationship with the other Bethlehem, in Palestine. I felt that something very significant must once have happened here.

Some villagers approached us. We were invited to the chief's guest hut, where we could rest and stay. Tafara spoke to them in Amharic and they all nodded understandingly. I suppose he gave them some indication of our mission. We were most hospitably received. Some women brought us a tasty brown stew and *thala*. The mules had plenty of hay and we rested. Then, at dawn, we would set off for Debra Tabor, and then on to Wehni Mountain.

When at last we were settled and alone, I asked Tafara to tell me some more about Prester John. He answered most eloquently. "Most literate Europeans in the Middle Ages knew about Prester John. They had heard about his letter written to the great Christian courts in the 12th century. He said he would assist the Crusaders in their war to free Jerusalem and the sacred places.

"They had heard about his empire, but were vague about where it really was. Marco Polo had confused him with the Tartars and obscured the issue. When Friar Jordanus wrote his *Mirabilia Descripta*, people began to accept that the center of Prester John's great empire may not be in Asia but further south, in the hot regions of East Africa – hence Abyssinia.

"The story was compounded further. In the Bible, it says in *Genesis* that the second of the four rivers that water the Garden of Eden is the Gihon... 'that compasseth the whole land of Ethiopia'.

"It may sound far-fetched, but Prester John knew all this, and possibly selected the region that was to be his center because it is close to the source of the Nile, and because *Jehon* is the Egyptian name for that river. Also, exactly contemporary with the growth of Prester John's fame in Europe was the emergence of the Grail cycle. In these legends the Grail is kept in a temple on the Mountain of Salvation. There lives the Grail King, the trusted keeper of the mysteries. This could have been our Mount Wehni."

Once again I was astonished by Tafara's learning. He told me he had made a study and earned a master's degree in his nation's mythological history at the university in Addis Ababa. We were both very tired and fell asleep at dusk.

When dawn broke, some villagers brought us a breakfast of cakes and hard-boiled eggs, served with their ubiquitous, delicious coffee. We said our goodbyes and thanked them for their generous hospitality. With more provisions and fresh water in our packs, we started the hazardous trek to Debra Tabor.

As we mounted our mules and started to move, an amazing event happened. Suddenly it was if my personal self, my sense of 'me', that I call Justin, just suddenly dropped away. Any feeling I had of separation with my surroundings was no longer there. I felt blissed out, in a sense of oneness and peace with everything around me. It was as if the landscape and the bodily form of Tafara were in an impersonal space which filled my whole being. I looked down and my body was in that space.

I was silent, dumbfounded for several minutes. Then my normal thought-stream returned. I had to tell Tafara about my experience.

"Yes," he laughed. "You have been given a free sample, my friend, of what is perhaps to come. Wait until we find Amhara and much more may happen."

I found his comments obscure but did not press the point.

"Yes," he said, "miracles happen here at Bethlehem. Remember, it was at the other Bethlehem that the three Magian kings came to worship the infant Jesus. At this Bethlehem, the Magi have also been present, through Prester John. Many saints and sages have spent years here in that old church. You caught something from their subtle leavings there, my friend."

As we trekked, Tafara entertained me by telling me some of the old Ethiopian proverbs. I remember a few. 'When you eat crow, call it pigeon.' 'One stone is enough against fifty clay pots.' 'You cannot build a house for last winter.' 'A good man earns more than his wages.' 'Even if you know many things, never argue with the judge.' 'The fool and the rich man can say what they please.' 'Do not try to taste honey if you see it on a thorn.'

We laughed a great deal and I told him some British proverbs. For some reason, 'There's more than one way to skin a cat' seemed to appeal to him greatly, along with 'Don't count your chickens until they're hatched'.

After a while we saw a sprawling mass of African huts spread out below the holy hill of Debra Tabor, sheltering its small town. Lively young children rushed out of their huts to greet us and escort us up the main street. On the top of Debris Mountain was a church, but we decided to rest outside in the open, near the marketplace. There we stocked up with provisions and then went to pitch our tents.

After cooking supper I again asked Tafara if there was anything else I should know about Prester John. He said that he would tell me, but not now, as we must get up at daybreak and head for Enfraz. There we would begin our search around Mount Wehni.

In the morning, after coffee and breakfast, we mounted the mules for the trek to Enfraz. Tafara said that Enfraz was a sizeable village and we slowly moved on, wafted along by a pine-scented breeze. We passed along a very good road for a while, the main route to Gondar. From the heights we could see the vast lake of Tana sparkling like a brilliant blue sapphire, 6,000 feet below us. I was stunned by the natural beauty all around. We didn't talk much, but en route I asked Tafara again for any final thoughts on Prester John.

Tafara replied, "There is no doubt that Prester John governed his huge empire wisely. We will never know the full extent of it. He spent some time in India and at Edessa in Syria, and a very long time in Ethiopia. Much of what we know about him is legend and he will probably always be an elusive figure who defies historical research – a bit like Jesus, if I may be so bold.

"There is much confusion about denoting India-greater, India-middle and plain India, when often they meant Abyssinia. Marco Polo was as much at fault as anyone. So let us forget speculation and pray patiently for revelation, if ever we stumble upon the entrance to Amhara, the true center of the sacred land of Prester John."

This seemed to be his last word, so I kept off the subject and enjoyed the rhythm of the mules' clopping along the metalled road to Enfraz. Apparently, in Mussolini's clownish adventure to take Abyssinia, Enfraz had been an Italian base. We reached the village by evening and pitched our tents by the market again so that we could stock up with provisions.

We dined well and shared the awe-inspiring silence under the stars. We both knew we were on the eve of a great adventure which would either end in fruitless fiasco or, as my guts kept on telling me, in some unknown discovery which would justify our bravado.

"Tomorrow," said Tafara somewhat solemnly, "we begin the trek towards Mount Wehni, in search of the Happy Valley. Hooray!"

In the morning, after a good breakfast washed down with the best Abyssinian coffee, we started on the climb to Wehni. The path, such as it was, rose steeply and was well-forested. Tafara suggested we might try to see if there was a path through the dense wood. We did find a rough path and entered.

The landscape we were now in was surrounded by mountain

peaks. The path went on for a while, seeming endless. Then, for some reason, the path seemed suddenly to finish in the middle of the forest and the mules halted, not sure how to proceed. Ahead it looked like a cavern that passed under a big rock. We decided to dismount and investigate on foot.

As we peered into the cavern beneath the rock, there was a rustle. A pair of large hands pushed out of the hole, holding a large cloth which was suddenly flung over both our faces. Tafara and I both fainted and evidently lost consciousness. I remember the smell on the cloth reminded me distinctly of chloroform.

When we recovered our senses, rather dazed, we found ourselves in a vast valley. A strong-looking, handsome young man warmly greeted us.

"Welcome," he said. "We knew you were both coming. You are now in Amhara, the sacred land of Prester John!"

There, spread out below in all its magnificent splendor, was the hidden Happy Valley, looking exactly as Dr. Johnson had described it in his *Rasselas*.

Chapter 6

Happy Valley

Some gracious valley embosomed in soft azureous hills
Smileth, an Eden as fair as God's love was feigned
To have planted for man's use-that lost garden regained.
From *The Testament of Beauty* by Robert Bridges III, 520.

Before we had time to fully recover from the surprise, our captor introduced himself.

"My name is Imlac."

I looked at him and had the presence of mind to say, "Imlac? Surely that was the name of Prince Rasselas' tutor in Johnson's book?"

"Yes." Imlac spoke beautiful English. "A strange coincidence, isn't it? It is a family name. Your Dr. Johnson did his research about Abyssinia very carefully before putting pen to paper. He was a most meticulous writer. Didn't he give you your first proper dictionary?"

"Yes indeed," I said, taken aback by this sudden burst of erudition. Tafara had recovered more quickly than I, and introduced us. "My name is Tafara and this is Justin, Justin Hart. We have been searching for the Happy Valley."

"Yes, we knew, so we made it easy for you."

By this time the side-effects of the chloroform were beginning to clear and I looked around at what I could see. It was a place of overwhelming natural beauty. But before I could take in any details, Imlac said, "Come, we must go first of all to the palace, where you shall be staying."

"Was this the palace of Prester John?" I asked, somewhat

hesitatingly.

"Yes, that is right. Incidentally, your mules have been tethered and are quite safe. Please use them if you wish to ride about in the vales of Amhara."

"Thank you," I said, not quite believing what I was seeing. But having pinched myself hard, I was assured it was not a sleeping dream.

"We shall now walk to the palace. It is only a short stroll."

His command of English intrigued me, but before asking a host of questions I just had to look around. The scene that now met my eyes was most impressive. I felt I could not really improve on Johnson's memorable description because it uncannily conformed with the apparent reality. There were high, well-forested mountains on every side. Sparkling rivulets seemed to be falling down many of the heights, irrigating the valley, which shone a bright emerald green.

It was obviously very fertile and filled with every kind of crop imaginable. I could see a large blue lake in the center of the valley and flocks of waterfowl hovering over clear, calm water. The mountains were covered with a variety of species of trees and mountain flowers. I could see pastures with goats, cattle and sheep grazing peacefully.

We approached what was obviously a palace, raised on a mound. The palace reminded me somewhat of the Taj Mahal in its symmetric, almost perfect beauty. It had one large central dome roofed in what appeared to be a copper-brass alloy. It glistened in the glorious sunshine. There were four spires on the four corners of the building. These spires reminded me of those on our cathedrals, but in perfect proportion to the dome. They were elegant fingers as if pointing directly at the heavens.

The building was faced with an almost translucent polished white marble which seemed to reflect the changing light patterns. Coptic carvings were sculpted around arched windows with multi-colored precious stones set in the marble, rather like the

Italian *pietra dura*. Everything proclaimed a total harmony and stillness.

We entered a porch which sheltered wide, exotically-carved rosewood doors, and we warily entered a large hall. The walls were of onyx and the hall was laid out with high-backed, carved mahogany chairs, as if for a lecture.

"You are now in the Prester John Academy, where we educate our young men and women," announced Imlac.

Extending the full length of the room on both sides were a number of red sandstone pillars. On each wall, engraved into the onyx, were the emblems of the zodiac, worked in gold and silver. At the eastern end of the hall was a huge representation of the sun, obviously made of solid gold. Both Tafara and I gasped, hardly containing our astonishment.

The room was lit by very large windows, arched at the top. They gave splendid panoramic views of the valley. The interior of the dome was azure blue, studded with gold representations of the constellations. There were large oil lamps shaped like flaming torches, placed at strategic positions around the hall. Although the floor was wooden, there was a tiled surround in a Coptic design. There were large numbers of woven carpets covering the floor, of the best antique type you used to find in Persia.

Tafara broke the silence. "So this is your school?"

"Yes, Prester John's palace is now mainly reserved for the education of our young people, in the principles of his wisdom. You see, Prester John governed his vast African empire, which reached to parts of India as well, by establishing philosopher-kings. This king or sage was the central figure underlying Plato's *Republic*, as you might know, but Prester John progressed this education with his synthetic knowledge, culled from many wisdom traditions, as well as from the ancient Greek. Here in Amhara the education of our people is the foremost priority."

Imlac looked at us sympathetically. "You both must be very

tired from your arduous journey and the strange shock of finding yourselves here. We have given you both guestrooms in the upstairs palace suite, as well as a sitting room in which to relax and enjoy your meals. Tomorrow I will come and visit you and we can talk. No doubt you will have many questions."

A youth then led us to our rooms up the broad staircase. Our luggage was laid out in separate bedrooms with adjoining bathrooms. There were extensive views out of the large picture windows. Both Tafara and I were so overwhelmed with fatigue and amazement that we did not know what to say to one another. So we retired to sleep.

In the morning I awoke to a golden dawn and a chorus of melodious birdsong. I dressed and went into the sitting room. The table was laid out with a splendid buffet breakfast. Tafara entered, then immediately after him came Imlac, dressed in the pure white cloak which seemed the common dress for most of the people I had seen. I noted they wore different colored turbans, burkas, scarves and waist bands, to break the uniformity. After we sat down and chatted a while, I asked Imlac how they knew we were searching for Amhara.

"Our knowledge of astrology is precise and accurate. We have scientific methods of prediction which has been proven over centuries. We have many finely-tuned sub-charts and we take the science much deeper than it is usually used, or may I say abused, in the West – but more of that another time.

"Our traveler chart showed us that at this precise time two men would be trying to find Amhara. Our scouts saw you approaching and picking you up was easy. It is very rare that anyone tries to find us now. The outside world seems to have forgotten about our existence and there is no tourist interest in this part of the country any more. This valley is hidden by high mountain ranges and can be entered only by one narrow gap beneath the rocks, and this is very well guarded.

"Yes, indeed, the magnetic force of destiny sent you both to learn about our civilization for some high purpose, no doubt. Once again the outside world, in its dire need for solutions to its problem of suffering, may be informed of our existence. We are in very dark times, we know that.

"We keep a scrupulous watch on the level of social corruption and cultural degeneration in the outside world. If a 'happy few', as your William Wordsworth used to say, know what we are attempting here, the world as a whole may benefit. After we have breakfasted, I shall take you to see some of Amhara."

We ate well and drank superb coffee. Then we sauntered out into the brilliant sunshine, accompanied by the ever-solicitous Imlac. There we bathed our eyes in the brilliant emerald green of the palace lawns. A simple, well-trodden path led us to the neighboring village. Here, well-built but simple huts contrasted vividly with the architectural harmony of the splendid academy.

"We are going to visit one of our families," said Imlac. We entered the spacious living interior of a large hut. The walls were beautifully decorated with colorful Coptic tapestries. All the necessary household utensils and basic necessities for living were there. A tall, well-built, handsome Abyssinian greeted us warmly.

"Good day. Men call me Haptu, and this is my dear wife Chiara."

These people struck me as so physically beautiful that I felt almost embarrassed, but there was nothing judgmental in their manner or demeanor.

"We have a baby and a young daughter, Simla, aged six, and Aaron our son is twelve. I am a farmer on the palace estate and my wife teaches at the village nursery school. Please take seats and then we shall enjoy some coffee."

We sat on low stools around a long, exquisitely-carved table of polished walnut. There was an open fireplace and a chimney reaching through the thatched roof. Chiara brought in some coffee beans. Then, putting them in a large iron ladle she lovingly held them over the hottest part of the fire until the beans crackled and jumped. Then she passed them round by holding the ladle near our noses for us to inhale the subtle aroma of the roasted beans.

At that moment Haptu lit some incense, which I recognized from my churchgoing days as frankincense. The two perfumes blended perfectly. Then Chiara took the beans and tipped them into a marbled pestle. She took a similarly marbled mortar and ground the beans to a fine powder. They were then tipped into a pot, with rapt attention, and the boiling water from a kettle on the fire was poured over the coffee grounds.

We sat silently for a moment. This making and serving of coffee was as sacred and important to them as a tea ceremony to any Japanese Zen monk. The liquid was then strained and served in small copper cups. It had a strong wine flavor. I felt my powers of cognition lifted and intensified by it to a point of discerning clarity. After the coffee was imbibed in silence, Imlac addressed us.

"Yes, Prester John felt very strongly and instinctively that the fundamental, harmoniously integrated family unit was the true basis of a good society. He knew this to be true from the ancient Laws of Manu and the Torah of Moses. He was a devotee of the Lord Jesus Christ, from whom he derived the spiritual inspiration of unconditional love and searching for the Kingdom of Heaven within.

"So, in Amhara, couples who fall in love with a view to marriage are free to do so. An accurate astrological chart is always made, showing their different tendencies and probable compatibility in the long term. They are advised by a skilled astrologer if there are likely to be any temperamental difficulties and what their future might hold. If they decide to proceed, which they generally do, then a marriage ceremony is arranged. Have you a question?"

"So Prester John believed in astrology, then?" I asked.

"Oh yes! He had studied very deeply the Chaldean, Babylonian, Greek, Egyptian and Vedic systems. He was a great synthesizer and he developed an accurate system of main charts and sub-charts that has an incredible accuracy, almost terrifyingly so, to answer any question put to the skilled astrologer. It is used here as a tool for making difficult decisions."

Tafara said, "You look a little skeptical, Justin, but it does work if you have enough information, I assure you."

"Yes," said Imlac. "We have lectures on astrology in the university, which you can come to if you wish."

"Yes," I said. "That would interest me a great deal."

"I will arrange it in good time," said Imlac. "So an auspicious marriage is arranged by the astrologer, and then counseling is also made available by the elders, and the wedding is sanctified by a priest."

"Who are these elders, then?" I asked.

"Our villages have approximately 2,000 souls each. Prester John believed this was the right number to form a dynamic church congregation. The elders, of which there are three in each village, are senior in age and graduates from the Academy. They can be either men or women, but never three of the same sex. Their role is to assist any village member who has any difficulty, in any field of activity, by giving sage advice. Each village is centered round its own church, assembly hall, nursery school, junior school and high school. The university is separate and has its own campus. There are necessary craft guilds for basic needs, a marketplace, an amphitheater, stables, steam baths and coffee houses. The assembly halls are available for celebrations, meetings, social events and so on."

"Worship?" I asked. "What about worship?"

"Prester John was essentially a very devout Christian emperor. He recognized the excellent virtues in all the traditional faiths. Comparative religion is a university subject here, and is also taught in schools at the appropriate age.

"Prester John received a powerful vision of the Lord Jesus when he was 13 years old. He fell in love with such pure spiritual beauty and unconditional love. He was also descended from a family of Magi, so he had access to the wisdom of Solomon as well. So worship, thanksgiving and sacraments, the joy of life which we see as God-given, is always available in the churches, where the priests hold open house all day and evening.

"But we must not digress. I wish to return to the basic idea of the harmonious family. Prester John held that we must always commence from our natural state. It is natural for the opposite sexes to wish to bring up children into this challenging world. In the early years, the children are brought up at home assisted by schools in the village. Prester John knew that the finest education possible was the essential key to a good society."

"So babies are brought up by their mothers, naturally?"

"Of course, but there is an underlying philosophy of love of wisdom behind all this," said Tafara.

"Of course," said Imlac. "Prester John saw human development as first of all a period when, about two years old, a healthy sense of ego or me-ness grows. This is inevitable and necessary for a sane capacity to handle the empirical, apparent world of the senses in which we live and have our being. Yet here is the big 'but', for Prester John knew that there was a second stage in the evolution of a developed, mature human being, when this ego or petty me-ness has to die for the full flowering of selfhood to flourish."

"Ah!" said Tafara. "This is the well-known, well-trodden mystical path to self-realization followed by all the higher religions and ancient mystery schools. Islam with her Sufism, Christianity with her monastic rule, and Gnosticism, the Jews with their Kabbalah, the Hindus with their Advaita Vedanta, the Buddhists with their Chan and Zen, and so on."

"Yes, Prester John was a Gnostic Christian and a Magus – he knew the wisdom of all these faiths. Representatives of these religions found their way to Amhara in his lifetime, and Prester John learned from them all, to evolve his own teaching with their added insights. So the child develops naturally. We have crèches for the babies to allow the mother some freedom for her own pursuits. Then infant school, junior preparatory schools, high schools, university and then the Academy, the jewel in the crown of Prester John's educational system in Amhara.

"Our life is built around education. A healthy ego grows, learning all the necessary skills, then we prepare for its eventual annihilation so selfhood may manifest in all its glory amongst our citizens. Now let us thank Haptu and Chiara for their excellent coffee and hospitality, and we shall all go and visit an infant school."

"I notice you have a beautiful Abyssinian cat here as a pet, Chiara?" I said. "Is that a common practice?"

"Yes, most families have cats. Like the ancient Egyptians, we discovered that they are such marvelous household pets. They are clean, spontaneous, self-contained and it is a joy to watch their grace of movement – besides which, they keep the mice at bay. The children love them."

We got up, said our goodbyes and walked in the direction of the village hall and to a nearby building, which Imlac said was the infant school.

All the public buildings were beautifully designed in the natural pink sandstone of the region, harmoniously proportioned with wide picture windows and interesting decorative features. I admired their symmetry.

"Yes," said Imlac, "these buildings are the work of our Guild of Masons and Architects, but later on we will tell you about our craft guilds, who manufacture for all our needs. Before we enter the school, remember that all the children have a general astrological chart and this is brought with them, along with their additional educational sub-chart."

We entered the infant school, a large bright room hung with

tapestries, but of a childish nature. I observed that these two-to-five year olds had every kind of playing opportunity you could possibly imagine. There were crayons, paints, blackboards, paper, wooden toys, linen books, sand tables, building blocks, board games, and soft balls galore.

"Now," said Imlac, "Chariana is one of the teachers here. I will let her explain."

"I am known here as Sister Chariana and my place is that of teacher of the village children from ages two to five. We have a very high ratio of trained teachers, one teacher to five pupils. This way, we get to know the children very well, forming a relationship based on love. Unconditional love is our guiding principle. The children are brought up without any fear of authority."

"What if they misbehave?" I asked.

"It is quite natural as the ego develops for a certain wild exuberance to come up, along with petty selfishness. So we sublimate these tendencies by having plenty of exciting games, dancing and sports. We try to see that the children are not frustrated in their expression, otherwise they can turn sour. If there is real naughtiness, then we hold their teacher responsible rather than the child. There is hardly any case we are unable to deal with intelligently – everything passes, and the so-called naughtiness is often the other end of the stick to impeccable behavior. We know, as Prester John taught, and by our own self-observation, that the psyche is based on opposites, so one charac-teristic balances another. Their astrological charts tell us all we need to know about these tendencies, so we can watch out for them and find a way to harness the energy to constructive use."

"Are all the teachers self-realized?" I asked with some trepi-dation.

"Not necessarily. You see, no one can get or achieve self-realization: it is a happening, an event, an understanding which descends through grace. The Academy prepares its students by giving them the correct intellectual concepts and support practices through which it may occur, God willing. Numerically, it probably only happens to 10% of the graduates, but nobody cares, since that is one of the conditions for enlightenment to happen. We like to have at least one member of staff who is enlightened in each school, because in the absence of the me-identification unconditional love flows through them to all the pupils."

"Thank you," I said, for that illuminating answer. "Who makes the appointments to the different schools?"

"It is left to the elders to accept any trained teacher who applies for their village school. It seems to work out exactly right – such is spontaneous serendipity in this best possible of all worlds."

I was beginning to wonder if we had not stumbled into some Kingdom of Heaven on Earth.

"Do you ever have problems?" I asked.

"Yes, God in His grace gives us problems to bring us closer to Him. Every difficulty is welcomed wholeheartedly. Overcoming any obstacle helps one jump higher next time one comes along. Prester John said there was no situation we were incapable of handling, and whatever happened was for the best and all was well, unfolding exactly as it should. In the infant schools, as in all the others, our doctors periodically check the children's sound physical development."

"What happens if a child becomes ill?" I asked.

"Oh, naturally the doctor is held responsible."

"Naturally," I answered. This seemed to be the approved word in Amhara.

"Where do they go to from your infant school?" I asked.

"Between five and eleven they go to junior school, which is preparatory for high school. Let us take a break now for lunch, and we will visit the junior school this afternoon."

We said farewell to Haptu and Chariana and returned to our

sitting-cum-dining room at the Academy, where a fine spread of Ethiopian dishes was laid out for us. They certainly have a splendid cuisine! We ate well, drank some delicious *teja*, and catnapped until Imlac came to take us to the junior school.

Leaving the palace by the path, I asked how Amhara could possibly afford such educational luxury.

"Well," said Imlac, "we are self-sufficient here and can manufacture as much produce and goods as each of our communities need. Everyone has the basic necessities of life. We need very little from the outside world and, if we do, someone goes out to buy it."

"Do you have money then?"

Imlac laughed. "We are sitting on the gold mines of the Queen of Sheba, but they are not exploited except for the odd purchase in the outside world."

"What about the people, don't they have money?"

He laughed again. "Heavens no, nobody wants or needs money here. The farmers bring their produce to the village market, as do the craft guilds. People take exactly what they need – no more, no less. No one has been conditioned to desire more than they can use.

"There is no need for money or private property ownership here. It is slavery to money that leads most people to spiritual bondage, which is associated with all the injustices, corruption and inequalities in the wider world. Man must feel free of this burden. Didn't Christ tell us that Divine Providence will supply all our needs? It certainly does so here, in abundance. But more of that later. Here is the junior school. Let me introduce you to Sister Yudit."

Sister Yudit was a striking and beautiful woman. Her features were pronounced and spoke of a spiritual maturity. She had large bright eyes, and she smiled and laughed almost all the time she was talking. I felt she must be one of the 'awakened' teachers. I could sense an energy which was almost palpable, containing so much warmth, interest and attention. At the same time I could recognize a spaciousness, as if there were no egotism inside this frame, but just intelligence and love.

"Our children are resting," she said laughing. "God bless them all."

Tafara asked her what they were trying to achieve. She laughed. "No one is trying to achieve anything – marvelous things just happen, like oranges appearing on orange trees, quite naturally."

"Naturally," I said, quite naturally of course. I was learning the local lingo.

Yudit continued, "We watch here for the tendencies we know from the astrological chart will be bound to emerge, and then we nourish those tendencies so that they flower. If they are frustrated they may become perverted."

"I'm interested to know," I said to Imlac, "how everyone speaks such beautiful English?"

"We love your language for its literature, its poetry, philosophy and fecundity of expression. It is the second language taught in our schools, alongside Amharic. It is now a universal language, so it is important for Academy graduates to know English fluently, if ever they are impelled to enter the outside world."

"How do you nourish the qualities you were talking about?" asked Tafara.

"Well, we feed and water them as they emerge. Let us imagine that we know from their charts that a certain child has a strong latent musical talent. As soon as he or she wants to play an instrument, a special program of musical education and encouragement comes into play. We have choirs and orchestras. We teach Western classical music, which is so harmonious, until some of your 20th century dissonant, minimalist divergences took over. We also have our own native Ethiopian and Coptic music. It is like this with every subject, be it mathematics, athletics, poetry, dance, theatre, history and so on..."

"Do you have problems with discipline, Sister?" I asked.

Sister Yudit laughed heartily. "What is indiscipline but a word? There is a certain wildness and rebellion in the children, and this is natural – it is the other end of its polar opposite, submission and conformity. So we have many sports and adventurous activities to encourage wildness to flourish. When it has expressed itself, the child returns to equilibrium. Anyway, the other children would never countenance one of their group behaving outrageously.

"There is great love and respect for each other and for their parents and teachers. Strong bonds are formed – it is very beautiful to see. Anyway, what is a problem but a God-given opportunity to learn from? I only wish we had more of them. It brings us closer to Him". She smiled, and her eyes twinkled.

Tafara was impressed. "Do you encourage sports?"

"Oh yes, every kind of athletic activity – soccer, hockey, rugby, tennis, golf, mountaineering, horse-riding and so on. There are not many sports that are not available here – somewhat on the English model." She laughed. "We even play cricket. It is a delightful game – it moves at the speed of life, there is a wonderful atmosphere of non-doing in it, and when the batsman or bowlers are on form it is like Zen, and they become one with bat and ball."

Her eyes lit up again. I could see she was clearly a cricket fan!

Imlac intervened. "Well, now you have some idea... Again the teacher-pupil ratio is very high, one to five. Tomorrow I shall take you to a high school. We must say goodbye to Sister Yudit now, as her classes will soon begin after the children's rest has finished."

"Thank you, Sister," I said. "It has been a great joy to meet you."

She hugged us all warmly in turn. I had never known such life-affirming exuberance.

As we left, Imlac said, "Tomorrow we visit a high school for adolescents from 13 to 18. This you will find most interesting. Now we shall return to the Academy. Please rest quietly, dine well and walk under the stars. I will call for you after breakfast and coffee tomorrow morning.

We followed Imlac's advice, as these astonishing experiences had made us somewhat tired and speechless. Next morning after daybreak, coffee and the dawn chorus, Imlac duly appeared.

We exchanged hugs. I began to see that this was the etiquette of Amhara, where so much love was flowing everywhere.

"We are going to the high school's hall now," he said. After a short walk we came to another architectural masterpiece and were greeted on the doorstep by a tall, dignified man of obvious weight and substance.

"This is Dr. Valentia," said Imlac. He and Dr. Valentia greeted each other like brothers and warmly embraced. I noticed that Tafara was much struck by the doctor – they appeared to resonate with one another in a mysterious way. They exchanged a long gaze, eyeball-to-eyeball, one to the other, without moving. This lasted a minute or two until Dr Valentia broke out into a broad smile.

"Welcome, and please come in."

We entered a large hall set out with elegant desks and chairs. There were more panoramic picture windows and interesting Coptic tapestries around the pink sandstone walls. At the far end of the room there was a semi-circle of chairs and a group of boys and girls in their mid-to-late teens were animatedly having some kind of discussion. These children were good-looking and handsome, with a radiant glow shining through their dark faces in a surprising way. They were talking in Amharic, so I did not know what they were saying to each other, except there was a great deal of laughter. No wonder this place was called 'Happy Valley'!

Dr. Valentia answered my question without my having to ask.

Perhaps he could read thoughts. "They are having a class meeting to discuss their next project, which is to be a detailed map of the villages around the Academy. This is the best way to get to know the different members of the community. Please come into my office so we may talk."

We entered the doctor's office. There was a simple desk with two chairs facing his own armchair. There was a bookcase and a wooden filing cabinet. There were some roses on a small table. Hanging on the pink walls was a fine portrait of Jesus. A most beautiful likeness with a compassionate smile, strong Semitic features and penetrating soulful eyes. There was a beard on the dark-skinned face.

Tafara opened the conversation with a question. "Why are you called 'doctor'?"

"Well, it so happens that I am a fully-qualified medical doctor as well as a trained teacher. In the adolescent school this is a great advantage, because in this difficult transitional period from childhood to adulthood there are often health problems because of the many changes that take place in the body."

"Are there psychological problems also?"

"Naturally enough," he said. "There are always problems of this kind in adolescence – a great many new powers are unleashed, both intellectual and emotional. There are many stirrings in the psyche. As teachers we must see that there is no confusion, and clarity is maintained. New energies are unfolding and of course the sexual inclination commences."

I could see this was going to be a very interesting discussion.

"Let us start with new energies," I said. "How do you handle the problems that teenagers have?"

"These often take the form of deep questionings, strong rebellion against the status quo, deep frustrations and so on. Here, because of a teacher-to-pupil relationship of one-to-five, we have ample opportunity to discuss all the difficulties. The pupil is encouraged to pour his heart out without fear or inhibition.

The teacher listens with pure attention and gives guidance when appropriate. This 'art of listening', without any resistance, allows the pupil to become aware of his own situation, and he often sees and hears that his resistance to actualities is the main problem. He may have to find a way of sublimating certain wild energies, as yet unstructured."

"Marvelous!" I said. "What about sex?"

"Ah," said the doctor. "The question with which you Westerners are obsessed, after centuries of repression. Here there is nothing hidden or forbidden. The whole question is tackled head on and explored with comprehensive relationship education. Generally we advise that a sexual relationship should complete itself in a sanctified marriage. This was the natural way that Prester John as a Gnostic Christian believed in. He knew that the family was the natural family unit."

"What happens if one of your pupils has an affair? Do you mind?"

"No, not at all. They are taught all about birth control. To have a child at this stage of their lives would be very difficult. If pupils fall in love and wish to experiment sexually, they are free to do so. Some do, many do not. It all just happens naturally, in the only way it can. We try to provide the young people with plenty of challenging adventure to sublimate this drive into creative channels."

"What about homosexuality or lesbianism?"

"Yes, we recognize that the male and female polarity exists in all humans. We hope that the natural faculty will win, but if it loses then it is accepted. Once people recognize bisexuality in themselves, they tend to opt for the richer relationship with the opposite sex. There are no rules here, and everyone loves everyone else, so if occasionally it manifests sexually, no one greatly cares.

"It is repression, guilt and shame which are the enemies of freedom and natural development. There is none of that with us here. Lust is born out of frustration or sex-starvation. Some young people have no interest and try to transcend the opposites, which they find rather coarse. Their energies are directed in more subtly refined ways, what you would call platonically. Anyway, we prepare them for adulthood, when they will meet the Tribunal."

"What Tribunal?" I appeared somewhat startled.

"Hasn't anyone told you about the Tribunal?"

"No."

"Well, there is a Tribunal or triumvirate of three elders in each village. Towards the end of their schooling they have an informal discussion with these three wise persons, two men to one woman for the boys, and reversed for the girls."

"What does the Tribunal do?"

The members of the Tribunal are the eldest of the awakened beings in the village. They study the astrological charts and receive an assessment of the child's learning skills. They try to discover from the child what he or she would ideally like to do for the first period of their adulthood – what they would really, really like to do. Once their vocation is expressed and ascertained, then the Tribunal advises on a program of further education.

"For example, if the child wishes to become a teacher, doctor, astrologer, farmer, artist, poet, writer or craftsman, philosopher, or whatever, he could well pass through the Academy, which is every citizen's right. We have most of the faculties known to higher education in our university – except, of course, finance and business, for which we have no need, along with political science.

"We have numerous craft guilds covering most hand-manufacture to a very high standard of workmanship and design. All the various objects to serve the basic needs of the society are available. Also we are independent of electricity in the main. We do, however, generate some power for our scientific departments in the university.

"All the domestic arts are included in our household and cookery schools. There is also a drama school, a college of music, an art college and a building skills department attached to the Masons' Guild. Prester John was very keen on masonry as the masons had learned the secrets of temple building from King Solomon. Your medieval cathedrals are great wonders of the world, so we study them to learn about the Knights Templars' understanding of sacred geometry, incorporated into our architectural school. We also have a mineralogy and mining department for the rare extraction of the Queen of Sheba's gold and other precious stones and metals."

"What about government?" I asked.

The doctor could hardly control his laughter. He seemed to find my question highly amusing. "Government! What government? The Academy prepares the great majority of our children through philosophy to learn true wisdom in the real sense.

"Each village community and educational institution is autonomous. There is no private ownership of land or property. All that is needed for an individual's welfare and development are gifts from the Tribunal in each village. All family needs are assessed. Educational institutions are similarly looked after and cared for."

Again I was astounded at what I had heard. "Come," said Imlac. "It is time for lunch. We will eat with the students, then we shall visit the Academy."

Over lunch I asked the doctor about religious education.

"Broadly you could say we are Gnostic Christians – that was Prester John's faith. But we are really beyond all labels. Prester John synthesized his knowledge and wisdom from the mystical traditions of the higher religions, so we give a general comparative religious background to all our children. We start from the external form and then lead on to the esoteric teaching.

"In the junior school they are told the wonderful story of Jesus and his parables. All seem to fall in love with this wonderful figure, who exemplified pure love. Of course many questions are asked which we try to answer to the student's satisfaction. But it is at the Academy that a truly religious education begins. The Academy is a wisdom school, and I suppose it is Amhara's main contribution to humanity. As you will find out."

"Yes," I said. "We shall be going there soon."

On the way back to the Academy, the doctor walked with us, and Tafara asked him to expand on the description of Prester John as a Christian Gnostic.

"Well, as by now you probably know, there have been numerous Christian Gnostic sects, all with varying shades of theological beliefs. The term means 'knowledge' from the ancient Greek *gnosis*. Prester John, as well as being a great Magus, borrowed many concepts from India, China, the early Christian Fathers, the Kabbalists and the Sufis.

"The Falashas are Ethiopia's own Jews, so he did not have to travel very far for their wisdom. There has been much confusion amongst scholars about Prester John's Indian connections, because Marco Polo referred to Ethiopia as Middle India. But Prester John did extend his empire into the Christian areas of India, founded by the early Apostle St. Thomas.

"Prester John was sought by the European Crusaders, to become their champion in their war against the Arabs, who occupied the holy places in Jerusalem. Although he offered support, he did not join in the war. Prester John realized that everything that happens in the universe emanates from Almighty God or the Source of Creation. He was holistic and non-dual in his philosophy. From his standpoint there was and is never anything else but God, which is synonymous with the transcendent, pure absolute consciousness-awareness-existence, which is the same as the immanent Self.

"You will learn all about this teaching in the Academy. He saw very clearly that mankind had separated himself from knowing God in himself, by falsely identifying with an illusory sense of separate individuality or egotism. A false sense of 'me' that believed it was the doer of all actions. But more of this when you visit the Academy.

"Prester John's heart was open and he loved God devotedly, whom he equated with his own self, the microcosm in the heart, mirroring the great divine macrocosm. God his Father, his Lord Jesus and the Holy Spirit were other terms for the Kingdom of Heaven inherent in the heart of every man and woman, as well as being transcendental powers. This Kingdom of Heaven inside us was to be rediscovered only if it was enquired into, as it was hidden behind thick clouds of egotism.

"Oh, we have reached the Academy already. We shall go to the lecture hall, where some of the principles underlying Prester John's form of Gnosticism will be taught."

We entered a long, large hall set out with elegant carved walnut chairs in semi-circular rows, ready for a lecture. There was a wooden platform on which stood a lectern, a small table, a vase of white lilies, and a flask of water. The walls were inlaid with white onyx and gold borders.

Imlac said, "This is our lecture hall, where those citizens who wish to come, with the assent of the Tribunal, may hear Prester John's esoteric doctrines. A lecture is about to begin in approximately half an hour, so please sit and wait."

Men and women started to enter the hall and sat down quietly. There was no talking, and a strong silence fell over the room. When the hall was full with about a hundred persons, Imlac himself rose from his chair and ascended the podium. To our surprise he was the lecturer. He spoke in English.

"Today," he said, "I shall give you some of Prester John's basic principles. Hearing them, a clear intellectual understanding of truth will enter your minds, if listened to with full attention. Eventually this will deepen as profound understanding, entering your hearts. This will clear the way for the possibility of the event of awakening to happen for you.

"First of all, we must see one fact very clearly. The truth cannot be explained or described adequately in words. As soon as the truth is stated verbally it falls down to the level of language, which is essentially dualistic in its organization and nature. Nevertheless it is the best we can do. Words can often be a barrier to understanding what in effect is a unique happening bestowed by the grace of God for enlightenment. So, in spite of the limitation of words, I shall have to use them." Mild laughter.

I was astonished at the look of happy attention written all over these serene and handsome black Abyssinian men and women's faces. All reflected composure and an eagerness to hear Imlac's oration.

"Are there any questions?" he asked, looking around the hall.

To my surprise it was Tafara who said, "Yes, please. If this teaching emerges from language, why can't we use it for its own description?"

"That is a very well-framed question, Tafara. Thank you. Now we must make it clear that this is Prester John's teaching, not mine. It came out of silence, revealed from the deep intuitive consciousness of the Self. It was not deduced by the brain using the tools of deductive logic or empiric reason. It did not come from language but out of the primeval silence, like the Word in the beginning.

"At the same time, we must recognize that language is necessary for human beings to communicate with each other, so we have to use it. It is the best we can do. Poetry may be better, but that comes later. Eventually we may communicate with each other through silence, so please trust me."

Tafara said, "Thank you," and looked as if a fog had lifted from his mind. Imlac continued.

"Principle two is this: truth resides in *what is*, and in the wholehearted acceptance of it." After a pause, Imlac expounded on this principle.

"*What is* means all that happens in the present moment. Everything ascertainable by one's awareness and senses is part of our holistic universe, where everything is interdependent on everything else. It is the inevitable necessarily ordained will of God, or the Source of Creation, or pure, absolute consciousness-awareness, the Self. Take your pick from whatever verbal symbol with which you best resonate.

"As the will of the Totality, it must be totally accepted as perfection emanating from the divine will. When this happens, there is harmony between you as a created being, a microcosm created in God's image, and the divine macrocosm. There is no division or separation. You are no longer bifurcated between a subject as 'me', and the world as an 'object'. Rather, the world is in you as pure awareness on your screen of consciousness.

"Involvement and identification with the conceptual 'me' and its programmed reactions cease. One only has to be tenderly aware at the point where attention touches the thoughts and feelings, which are reactions from your mind. You can simultaneously witness this happening and be aware of whatever occurs in consciousness, inside and outside the skin. Are there any questions so far?"

The deeply attentive audience seemed to have been stunned into silence by Imlac's oratory, which was punctuated by long silences and sounded quite oracular. I suppose we were all assimilating his words and letting them sink in before reacting with a question at this stage.

Imlac continued. "I shall tell you the next principle. Truth resides in *what is* at any moment, and in the wholehearted acceptance of it. Always bear in mind that every word Prester John said about truth can only be a pointer or signpost to it." He paused.

"That is all I am going to say this morning. There is enough to digest and to ponder on. We shall resume tomorrow afternoon.

Meanwhile, don't think too much about what I have told you. If you have been listening with attention, then the taking in of these ideas or concepts will do the work on their own, in a very natural way, in their own time. Now let us sit together in silence for ten minutes."

The hall was electric with the vibrant energy of these meditating consciousnesses, pondering silently. It was almost palpable, the love and the silence. After what seemed a short time, Imlac rose, smiled and left the podium. The students slowly filed out of the hall in an orderly way. Imlac came over to us and, smiling, said that he would take us to see one of the guilds this afternoon.

Chapter 7

We Visit a Guild

A damsel with a dulcimer
In a vision once I saw:
It was an Abyssinian maid,
And on her dulcimer she played
Singing of Mount Amara.
Could I revive within me
Her symphony and song,
To such a deep delight 'twould win me,
That with music loud and long,
I would build that dome in air,
That sunny dome! Those caves of ice!
And all should cry, Beware! Beware!
His flashing eyes, his floating hair!
Weave a circle round him thrice,
And close your eyes with holy dread,
For he on honey-dew hath fed,
And drunk the milk of Paradise.
Samuel Taylor Coleridge, from *Kubla Khan*

After our splendid buffet lunch and time for resting, Imlac called for us at our living room in the Academy. As we walked down the path, Imlac explained that the craft guild system was the basis of Amhara's economy. Imlac told us that as the young Ethiopians developed, many informed the Tribunal that they would like to follow a career in one of the many craft guilds.

"Most citizens of Amhara have at one time or another worked

57

in one of the guilds," said Imlac. "For a while I was a potter."

"Today," he said, "we shall visit the Weavers' Guild." We soon arrived at a group of purpose-built sheds surrounding what was a main hall. We entered and again I noticed an invocatory poem in both Amharic and English engraved on the stone. I noted it down.

The Unseen Weaver

There's a huge loom of time, in duration;
Born of infinity, from a consummation
With life, which has never been void of time,
While sun and moon as shuttle upward climb.

By weaving to and fro as night and day,
A splendid pageant of coloured display,
Strung on the warp and weft of unity.
The back of this embroidered tapestry

Is monochrome, derived from the formless One.
Its face is multihued, radiant as the sun;
Its tones reflected from archetypal light,
Are magically absorbed, an unequalled sight.

Only what's permitted by an unseen hand,
Appears on this moving panoramic band;
A rainbow painting of the whole wide world,
Brushed vertically; each single thread is whirled

Without the dimmest dint of dull duality;
Bright light, unique to Self, sheer reality!
Coated with golden fleece and angel's wool,
Dyed in the deepest vat of destiny's pool.

So does this sacred cloth, woven in love,
Quarrel with its weaver who rules above?
Wrapped in his Joseph cloak at rainbow's end,
Eternal pilgrim ever loves his Mighty Friend.

I was most impressed by the power of these simple verses. I said to Imlac that sometime he should tell us about their poetry school, if they had one.

"Oh yes," he answered. "In the university and all through the educational system, poetry and prosody are favored subjects. I will tell you about it and how much we value the art of translation, so that the Amharic verses can be expressed in English – and vice-versa. But more of that later. Here comes Absolem, the head weaver."

Imlac introduced us to a fine, well-built, middle-aged Ethiopian with bright eyes and an engaging smile. Laughter lines flickered up and down his face. He and Imlac embraced like brothers and he greeted us with obvious affection. Again I felt a transmission of something other than personality which we are so used to in the West that can only be described as *presence*.

He was sending a message to me like an invisible arrow from heart to heart, an arrow of love fired from an emptiness that contained everything but emanated from nothing. Yes, 'presence' was the closest word I can find to describe the impact that this extraordinary being made on me.

Absolem took us first of all to some fields where they grow the plants necessary to make the vegetable dyes. There I saw madder, indigo, woad, safflower and many other herbs I could not recognize, given my limited botanical knowledge. It was a very beautiful herb garden.

"From these herbs we can obtain most colors if we use the right mordants," he said. "Often the roots, when dried, are ground into pigments and powders."

Next to the garden there were huge vats tended by young

apprentices, who were dipping different textiles into them. There were hanks of wool, cotton and flax hanging from spikes all around. The colors were radiant like the rainbow. Next door was the designing room. Here young men and women were working at large tables painting designs on large squared graph paper, and deciding the colors to use for whatever the weave determined. I was impressed by the grace and fluidity of the designs, which seemed to flow like water and were obviously inspired by nature.

Then we went to the spinning room, where girls and boys sat by spinning wheels. I thought Mahatma Gandhi would have been very pleased to see this. At last someone was living his principles of village craft industry. We stopped in the weaving rooms where huge looms were being worked backwards and forwards by foot treadle shuttles.

Absolem told us, "The Carpentry Guild makes these looms for us. All the guilds serve each others' needs. In this way we are self-sufficient."

In the weaving room Tafara asked about the principles involved.

"Ah!" said Absolem. "Prester John held that all the crafts were primarily a training in undivided attention. Here we learn to use the mind correctly as a working instrument, highly skilled on the empirical level. When this working mind is attentive, it is not able to wander about like a crazy monkey, backwards and forwards in the graveyard of the past or into the fantasy of an imaginary future which may never happen. This type of conceptual thinking is a dreadful waste of energy and leads to psychological suffering.

"All our students rotate into the different rooms of the weaving schools until each is a master of every sub-division in his or her own right. The rugs and fabrics are made for the needs of the community or for other institutions. Each community or grouping of villages has its own Weaving Guild, as it does for the other crafts, according to their needs. Nobody owns anything here or is obliged to remain, and are they free to move to other crafts whenever they feel the need.

"This move is discussed with the Tribunal and their astrology is checked to see that there is no danger for them lurking anywhere. This system has created many fine artists and some beautiful art. We also teach the philosophic principles of Prester John's wisdom, as they do in the Academy – and now many of our weavers are inwardly liberated!"

"Yes," said Tafara. "Your weavers look idyllically happy."

"They should indeed!" said Absolem, smiling. "After all, this is not known as 'Happy Valley' for nothing!"

"Yes," said Imlac. "We have very many different craft guilds like this. Please feel free to visit any you want. The weavers also serve the Tailors' Guild, who cut and sew our cloaks, scarves and turbans".

What a joy, I thought – no heavy industry, no pollution, no discontented wage-slaves, no exploitation, just fulfilled human beings. What a paradise!

Absolem said that each craft tries to find the inner significance of its craft. "The weavers see their craft as a good metaphor for Creation, where space and time are the looms, the Sun and Moon the shuttle, and all the garments are illusions woven in light."

"Yes," I said, "how beautiful. And how about the tailors?"

"For them each stitch unites the being with the Earth and Heaven."

Absolem then said farewell to us, as he was going to give a talk to some of the dyeing students on the finer points of mineral mordants. We embraced warmly, and we thanked him for his hospitality. Again I felt an arrow of love shot into my heart. His gaze into my eyes seemed to evoke some sense of selfhood in me which transcended my ordinary reactions and emotions.

Imlac led us away. Now I was determined to ask him about

the poetry schools, so impressed was I with what I had read as an invocation here.

Chapter 8

Poetry

The Queen of Sheba said: "Know, my nobles, that I have received a gracious message. It is from Solomon and reads as follows: "In the name of Allah, the Compassionate, the Merciful.

Do not exalt yourselves above me, but come to me in all submission."

The Prophet Mohammed, *Koran* 27:23

Imlac answered my question about the poetry schools as we were strolling back to the Academy. He began by telling me that poetry was of special interest to the people of Amhara, taught throughout the educational system, culminating in the university.

He said, "In the university there is a department of English as well as of Amharic literature. The people here love English, the *lingua franca* of contemporary mankind. It is so rich in vocabulary, offering so many possibilities of expression. We see it as a great field for the unfolding of poetic possibilities.

"We read your great writers. Everyone here appreciates the plays of Shakespeare. We study and admire poets such as Shelley, Keats, Byron, Browning, Tennyson, Swinburne, Traherne, Whitman, the two Rossettis and Eliot. The list is endless. Many wish to write too, so they are taught the fundamentals of English prosody in the high school. As their philosophical understanding develops and their narcissistic egotism gets diminished, the muse inevitably shines through them.

"We believe in the musicality of poetry. We love it to sing and really appreciate the use of rhyme, meter and form. We love figures of speech such as assonance and alliteration, and we admire free verse when it is rhythmically crafted and inspired – not just spun off the top of the head as prose broken up into lines. Our poetry follows the guidance of Shelley in his marvelous essay *The Defence of Poetry*, where he talks about a higher poetry.

"We think the subject matter of poetry should point to man's spiritual evolution and noblest aspirations. We also think highly of the Indian poets Tagore and Aurobindo. Of course we study the best translations of the mystical poets from all the religious traditions such as St. John of the Cross, Rumi, ibn Gabirol, Blake, and so on – what a galaxy! A real gift from God, like music and all the arts."

"Have you any examples you can show me of your English poetry?" I asked. "I suppose you also study the art of translating your best Amharic works into English?"

"Yes, we do. We have a literary magazine devoted to poetry, circulated to all citizens. I will give you a copy. Our Printers Guild and Bookbinders Guild work closely with the poetry workshops in the university."

"Thank you," I said. "I shall look forward to reading some."

"Good. We will now detour to the bookbinding shed and collect one now."

We entered the shed and Imlac asked for a current issue of *The Happy Valley Poets*. It was beautifully designed and printed. I read through it that evening and found some delightful poems. Here are a few examples.

EGOECHTEMY
The laser beam of finely-honed attention
Dives inward, with breath and thought retention,
Searching for the source of 'phantom me'.
It cuts through five sheaths and veils we see
Of habits, thought forms and selfish will,
Formed over many lifetime dreams, so ill.

The Pearl Fisher finds nothing on the floor
Of his deep interior ocean bed, no more;
Then one time, his mind drops in his heart,
He finds his ego, and it falls apart.
Crash, crash, it topples, shakes, then falls down.
The Ganglion Knot's been severed at its crown.
Open heart surgery has been performed,
The errant soul no longer quakes, deformed.

A SONG OF UNITY

I am full as a mountain lake after the summer rain
That's fed the sacred stream and source of holy wisdom, love.
A fire sent by God to ignite His planet, from above.
The golden glow of heat on burnished plain
Gilding leaves on this march down pilgrim's lane;
Warming the earth, her gritty ochre clay,
Water, sea of mercy, so green and grey.
Air, the sweet breath of life that's free from pain,
Crystalline, beyond any loss or gain.
What does it mean to my Master, pure as a turtle dove?
This vast empty void, a deep abyss, the precious pearl
Of trial that poor pilgrim has to pay.

What of scripture, tracts, gospels and theological books?
The Lord's lurid library of commands and revelation;
A crore of scribbling comments with endless emendation,
Weighty tomes which cram cathedrals nook and crook
To surfeit, cawing like a craw of rooks.
What is self-knowledge, esoteric?
Pathology of mind, narcissistic?
Even when freed from the senses it looks
A hotchpotch prepared by the devil's cooks;
To titillate the senses to some novel sensation.
So what is freedom, vulgarised by folk-democratic?

But my Master who is One is truly aristocratic!

What is knowledge of truth, understanding, enlightenment
And ignorance, sleep, alienation, dark delusion
Or folly, dithering in a dream of world illusion?
Or freedom from bondage and attachment?
Are these questions the prime predicament?
What means ego? I thought, I conceit
Imprisoned by mind, one beds in self-deceit,
This is mine, a grasping temperament
For baubles, attractive but so vehement?
Or the form of self-consciousness to save from confusion,
To rescue soul from duality, its preordained defeat?
I pray for grace and mercy at my Master's tender feet.

I am without a central 'I-notion' resident at home,
There's no me to be elated or badly hurt by fear,
Pleased, perplexed, precious, pouting, proud, or simply here
To feel depressed, anxious. A soul free to roam
On inward seascape of bubbles, froth and foam.
So where is he who suffers, enjoys, acts,
Who has strong opinions and knows all facts?
The rising of thoughts under a cerebral dome,
What's this world? The trinket of an impish gnome?
Here and now there's no fictional person to jeer or leer,
For my Master, Dame Fortune's cards are neatly dealt in
stacks,
Abidance in the heart, Real Self, no need for lofty tracts.

Seated in the temple shrine of the spiritual heart
Nestling on the dexter side of my heaving breast
Not on the left where the fleshly pump pulses in the chest,
Dwells 'I Am' which wakens Self to start.
Pondering, I question, what is the part

I play on life's stage and what is this world?
Who yearns for freedom from prison where hurled?
Oh what is oneness, truth and wisdom's art?
Into which God shot love's rose-flowered dart?
Who is bound or free as the honoured friend and conscious
guest?
Behind the nervous body-mind and now at last unfurled,
Space for a universe to happen in, lustrous and impearled.

Deep in my spiritual Heart, I am the One, unborn,
Uncaused, deathless, I am, uniquely perfect, new, absolutely
free!
I ask what is this tempestuous, stormy, troubled sea?
Where froth foams spuming from dusk to dawn,
On the ocean of Self lit by a fiery morn.
What is creation, world dissolution?
I ponder, and search for some solution.
Who and what is seeking? King, bishop or pawn
On this chequered emerald palace lawn?
What is the goal of seeking? Is it peace, freedom, liberty?
Who is the bold seeker who craves this final absolution?
Has he found any answer? An ultimate resolution!

I am pristine, pure as the driven Abyssinian snow
As a pellucid stream pouring from a pinnacle's height,
Chaste, flawless, stainless, without blame, blemish and
wintry white.
I trickle down the mountain valley's flow
Free! I'm curious, what is there to know?
By what dubious method is knowledge gained,
To what spurious end when it's attained?
I have no problems here, now or there below,
I've surmounted grief, all sorrow born of woe,
Simply stated, I know what is meant by both wrong and right.

Our universe by creation, preservation, is maintained
By grace of God and his mighty will, all creatures are
sustained.

Here, awakened now, I am steady and perfectly still
As an adamantine rock in the restless ocean stands,
Unmoved by cyclonic gale, tidal wave or shifting sands,
What of oppositions, healthy or ill,
Pleasure, pain, to heal quickly or to kill;
Distraction, perturbation, meditation,
Reflection, negation, confirmation?
Sage welcomes all as God's almighty will
He accepts 'what is', as gracious grist to his mill.
Gently by grace of God, in mercy, he breaks all bondage bonds
In a great paean of praise and total affirmation
He rests with consciousness, his Self, the great consummation.

I have lost the monotonous merry-go-round of thought
The perpetual treadmill of self-opinion and words,
Mainly cynicism and lies, the parroting chirp of birds,
A poisonous brew so bitterly fraught
With the mistaken idea that I ought
To cherish the mind as chief.
Am I to be mugged by thought, the villainous thief?
So that is the lesson my dear Master brought,
Ignore the scorpion stings of concepts wrought
With this inner discussion and debate. It's so absurd
There is consciousness here, a gift beyond any belief
And the ending of thought; peace, ultimate joy and relief.

I am clarity pure as diamond, crystal, lily-white
Growing in a moorland, a purple thistle-bracken field.
So what is illusion? To this question I meekly yield.
Finite mind can't understand the infinite,

And magic of Maya is but a slick trick of light.
What is this life? A bad dream which appears?
A note to deceive the soundest of ears,
An emptiness as velvet void as night
For witnessing Self, nakedness of clear inward sight.
To know what is here now beyond pearl onion peeled.
So my Master gently wipes away all my sad grief and tears,
All is well, unfolding as it should to allay foolish fears.

With not the slightest hint of duality, One without two,
Unity, wholeness, existence, holistic, all seamless
Without separation, pure consciousness, love, awareness,
No division between me and you
Emanating from the Primal Source, who
Am I, but That? I am eternal, the same
Being as truth and God without a name.
At last I know the little 'me' who can never do,
All that happens is the will of God right through.
I rest in the spiritual heart, blissful, benign and blameless,
So what is my greater Self to the mighty God of flame?
My Master says "Unknown, unique, celebrate His game.

"For endless striving and effort, what's the urgent need?
Struggling, wrestling against one's natural way and feeling
Trained from the cradle to do well, and practice honest dealing,
Working hard if you wish to barely feed
A family own home, car and succeed,
Ingrained, conditioned, a machine well oiled,
Pilgrim's become half-baked and par-boiled".
So my Master to his students does plead,
Be still, motiveless when you perform any deed.
So forget all those books, aims, efforts, teaching and kneeling,
After all the hard years you've zealously worked and toiled

Open wide, relax, and never by the world be coiled!

I have no limits or borders, I am no longer bound.
No more hedges, fences, verges, remain for spacious me,
Nothing arises, I am empty capacity for all to see
That all is well, my True Self I have found!
I traced my 'I thought' like a hunting hound
And knew my primal source, the light of day,
And now as consciousness I'm free to play.
I rest in the heart on a sacred mound
Where my naked feet walk on holy ground.
I am freedom, enlightenment, joy, bliss and liberty!
Nothing ever was, I am God, what more is left to say?
This Prester John taught me, his devoted pupil, the true
Amharic way!

I am That, absolute, unique, ever primeval One
As consciousness, love, awareness, effortless bliss,
Embraced by the love of God, blest by His all-gracious kiss ;
In light of glory, radiant as the sun,
I am homogeneous, second to none.
What care I for freedom or liberation?
In life or death, gaining realisation?
Or for my destiny predisposed to run,
Reborn in another womb till kingdom come?
And after transmigration, at-one-ment I may miss.
My Master halts this baffling mental perturbation.
I let go, abiding in my heart of silent adoration.

This was quite a poem. I felt like someone's attempt at a major
work. I was intrigued by the complex stanza structure with its
interweaving rhyme endings and longer lines framing the
pentameters. Their school seemed quite advanced. I read on.

The poems were all unsigned, so anonymity was preferred to the egotistic craving for name and fame. I suppose all the craft and artist guilds left their works unsigned, as was common in the medieval period, for similar reasons. And one other, a sonnet.

ROSE GARDEN
In the radiant rose garden of my heart,
In my sunny summertime of meditation
On God's name: by steady concentration,
The white lilies of devotion impart
Their scent, welcoming an earnest start
To prune the growths of grief and dissipation,
Heralding the dawn of firm mental regulation.
Then worship blooms to form a sacred part
Of hymnal chants that I sing in adoration.

The sweet apple of self-knowledge and bliss,
Pure awareness, is a joyful fruit
Sealed with the Divine Mother's loving kiss,
She fulfils the magic of my self-pursuit.
Bold beauty adorns my bower of peace,
In the ardent arbour of my soul's release.

There was no time to read any more, although I was keen to do so. I was due to return to the Academy at the university, for a second lecture on Prester John's teaching. I was so impressed by this beautiful poetry. How much better, I thought, than that contemporary verse back home with its mundane subjects, most of which read like prose with line breaks. No wonder it is unpopular and the public prefer the Victorian Romantics.

Their poetry reminded me of Shelley's saying in his *Defence of Poetry* that a great poem was like a loving fountain of delight and wisdom. What a joy this Amharic poetry is, so very modern, and in English too!

When I returned to the Academy for the next lecture I sat down beside Tafara as before. Imlac started by restating the next principle.

"The understanding of truth can only happen when the mind is empty of all thought and all conceptualization. Now, enlightenment happens mainly by the grace of God, or pure consciousness, Self, awareness, love, the Totality – call it by any name which resonates best for you. It is 'That' which does everything, the one sole doer, the source of the ego in the spiritual heart, in the right side of the chest. Not in the fleshy pump on the left.

"The mind must be free and empty of its wandering tendency to move backwards or forwards in imagined time, from past to future, instead of keeping still in the present. This wandering thought-stream we call 'conceptualization', the subjective checking of everything by previously-held belief systems and continuous self-referencing. In a single word, 'thought' or 'mind'. All these habits have to be dropped and let go of. Now, have you any questions?"

At this point I was impelled to speak. "Surely," I asked, "There is a place for effort at the beginning of the quest, in order to become focused?"

"Yes indeed", said Imlac. "That is a good question, and it shows some maturity. If you are impelled to make effort by God's will, then nothing can stop it. Pray for it to happen! Yearn for it! You must practice self-enquiry! This is the great necessary effort and the next principle." His voice rose to emphasize the point.

"You must turn inwards, 180 degrees, and probe skillfully like a good surgeon beneath the skin, searching deeply into the spiritual heart to find the ego's source. Then it will topple and die. But great persistence and determination are needed for this essential effort. It must be repeated over and over again, possibly for years. This is Self Enquiry, or put it another way Enquiry into the Self. By Self we mean the essential 'I Am-ness' inherent in every man or woman. When Moses asked God his name, God replied I AM THAT I AM. It is plain as a pikestaff as we say here. You can also call it The Space of Pure Awareness dwelling in the cave of your spiritual heart. When you are able to abide in that, and just 'Be Still' as King David said you will know that I am God. This is what Jesus meant when he said "I Am is the way and the life. Prester John used the word Self because he knew the Upanishads and he had reached the same position as your Bill Shakespeare when he wrote 'This above all to thine own Self be true'!

Wow, I thought, I was privileged, I had never known anything put so clearly as this and I had been attending spiritual groups on and off for donkey's years.

"Of course," said Imlac, "Prester John was adamant that the spiritual heart was on the right side of the chest. He knew this from his personal experience when he dived inwards to discover his True Nature, who he really, really was, in fact."

He paused in a silence which lasted a couple of minutes during which I felt deeply moved, then he continued. "Don't ever *think* about progress either. Real progress happens when you stop thinking about making progress. All your egotistic latent tendencies have accumulated over this and many lifetimes, and will mercifully emerge with Self Enquiry. This obscuration, clouding your Real Self, will be removed. The sun of the Self, which is pure consciousness-awareness-reality-bliss, will shine through.

"The complex of nerves forming a ganglion knot connecting you to an identification with your body and mind will be broken once and for all. This is freedom. This is liberation. But first you must have unconditionally surrendered to the divine will and earnestly practice Self Enquiry. That will create the condition for self-realization to happen, if it pleases the Almighty, or the Self, your inner teacher, the inner ruler in your heart. Are there any further questions?"

The hall was silent. You could have heard a pin drop.

"Good," said Imlac. "This is an auspicious sign, when the mind has ceased its contention. But whenever you need clarification, please do ask."

"The next principle is this. When enlightenment, self-realization comes, it will arrive suddenly, when least expected. Awakening happens unplanned, out of the blue. It is an event ordained by the grace of God. You suffered from a bellyache, and suddenly it is gone. There is no egotism left anywhere, in the sense of a personal, self-centered 'little me'.

"Self-referencing and continuous commenting and criticizing on the basis of 'I like' or 'I dislike' stop. There is a fundamental shift in perspective from duality, from 'me and the world', to non-duality, where there is no longer a sense of separation between one's essential I Am-ness and the world. Now, I am the world and the world is in 'I'."

There were again no questions. I felt I had been given the highest teaching common to the great mystics of all the great religions.

"Finally," said Imlac, "when it happens, it cannot be accepted unless the mind is empty of the 'me' and the heart is full of love.

"Are there any further questions?"

A young man said, "Surely, when the 'me' goes, love enters in as a matter of course, naturally? I had a taste of that. Then it left."

Imlac replied, "Yes, you are quite right. You received a taste of awakening – that is, grace. This often happens before a more intense or deeper happening, when it becomes unmistakable and stabilizes".

A young lady asked if an event was always necessary.

"Yes, in every case. Each one of you is unique, a force field of energy in process. You are not separate individuals, as you have been tricked by the senses to believe. You are each sitting there at the center of the universe, as that consciousness in which a world seems to appear – a magic picture show. So there are no absolute rules about what may or may not happen, only pointers and ground rules.

"Any further questions? No? Then we shall resume tomorrow. Let us sit in silence and meditate together for twenty minutes."

After the deep and penetrating silence, the hall emptied and I started to wonder if I was totally happy about the Happy Valley. This is a utopia, a bed of roses without thorns, of life without much struggle or suffering. Not like the other world, where I came from.

Hadn't Prince Rasselas had similar doubts when he escaped to Egypt from the Happy Valley? Like the Buddha, he wanted to see worldly suffering and find the way to remedy it. Rasselas found no lasting happiness there, alas – only an ability to endure. I would have to enquire with Imlac about my doubts.

"Imlac," I asked, as we strolled back. "I have some doubts, wonderful as all this is…"

"Yes," replied Imlac. "The monkey-mind thrives on doubts. Remove one doubt and another will take its place. But please go on."

"Surely this life here is too perfect? There is no suffering, which can assist growth, development and developing nobility of character."

"Ennoblement follows quite naturally after realization. Admittedly, the suffering here is small in comparison to the mechanical pain-factory of the ordinary world. But Prester John's Amhara was not founded merely to create a utopia. Admittedly, as a utopia it may serve as a model for a new society after the other one collapses, as it inevitably will. But the aim is much greater than that."

"What is that aim, then?" I asked.

"Our aim is to create a model of a social environment in which the human being can flower to his or her full potential, fully awaken, and then enter your terrifying ordinary world and assist it by raising the general level of awareness – or at least, mitigating the effects of the worst degradation and corruption."

"You mean, like some *homme inconnu,* or 'hidden and just men', or the Kabbalistic Zadik?"

"Yes, something along those lines. After self-realization and its deepening and maturation, graduates of the Academy are sent secretly to dark places on the planet. They bring light and perhaps help restore the righteous balance of a just harmony. This brings them suffering at first but is very soon surmounted. But more of that later."

"But how do they get out of here?"

"Exactly the same way as you came in – secretly. They trek to Addis Ababa and can then travel by air to wherever they are destined to go – very well equipped, believe me."

Tafara was obviously visibly moved, almost to tears, by such a revelation. I wondered whether he had met one of them, without knowing it.

"Now," said Imlac, "after lunching we shall visit the university."

Chapter 9

The University

Ethiopia shall soon stretch out her hands unto God.
Psalms of King David, LVIII, v31

After lunch we had a good rest. It was necessary to digest the buffet of traditional Abyssinian delicacies, one of the finest cuisines in the world. Imlac called for us and we started to walk. Soon down a well-made path, we approached a large complex of quadrangular buildings, with arched windows, turrets, domes and spires.

It had quite a magical appearance. There were groves and avenues of trees sited all around the pink-washed buildings. There were colorful flower beds, fountains and emerald green lawns. I suppose they had a Gardeners' Guild too. Inside the first college we entered, there was a quadrangular cloister enclosed by what were obviously residential halls and lecture rooms. The buildings were two-storied and linked by staircases which looked out through glass windows onto the distant fields and snow-capped mountains enclosing Amhara from the outside world. Young people in white garments and brightly colored turbans, burkas and scarves thronged the campus.

Imlac told us that the university served a number of villages. The village communities sometimes linked into groups for different purposes such as higher education and certain specialized guild activities. The universities were available to whomever wished to attend after discussion with their Tribunal. One was free to change courses with their consultation and even to resume again years later.

"Now which department shall we visit first?" asked Imlac.

"How about music?" said Tafara. I agreed.

Imlac informed us that the music department was divided into three sections, that of Western classical music, Ethiopian Coptic traditional music and sacred world music.

At the Traditional Music College we were greeted by Sister Sarah, a well-built, contented looking lady dressed in traditional Abyssinian regalia. Imlac and Sister Sarah embraced warmly and I could sense the impersonal love which was so much part of the Amhara environment, flowing strongly between them.

"Tell them, Sister," said Imlac, "about our music."

Sister Sarah took us inside the college. I could see a concert hall and many ancient instruments stored against the wall. I could hear chanting being practiced, dimly echoing from different rooms. We went into a sitting room which seemed to be an extended office for Sister Sarah.

After we sat down she told us that Ethiopian sacred music started with a certain St. Yared. Apparently he learned composition by listening directly to birdsong, something like our Messian, I thought. These were God's own musical creatures and, noting their melodies and harmonies by careful, attentive observation, he deduced a wealth of musical knowledge.

As we were speaking, her words were accompanied by a young man lightly tapping a large drum. It seemed to come from the concert hall. Coincidentally, the drumming seemed to underline her words. I could see the drummer from where I was sitting, through the open door. The drum hung from his shoulders and was cone-shaped, stretching from neck to waist. He beat it gently at both ends with either hand.

"Now," said Sister Sarah, "let me show you some words we have emblazoned on the concert hall wall, relating to his musical approach."

We entered the concert hall and I read the following.

"Now in those days there was no singing of hymns and

spiritual songs in a loud voice to well-defined tunes. Men murmured them in a low voice. God, wishing to raise up to Himself a memorial, sent unto Yared three birds from the Garden of Eden. They held converse with Yared in the speech of man. They caught him up and took him to the heavenly Jerusalem, and there he learned the songs of the Four-and-Twenty Priests of Heaven."

"Of course," said Tafara. "Many medieval scholars such as St. Bonaventura believed that the Garden of Eden was in Abyssinia."

"Yes," said Sister Sarah. "Many of us feel strongly that Amhara is the actual site."

It certainly seemed a probability, judging by what was going on here, I thought. I continued reading the wall text aloud.

"And when he returned to himself, he went into the First Church in Axum, at the third hour of the day, and he cried out with a loud voice, saying 'Hallelujah to the Father, hallelujah to the Son, hallelujah to the Holy Spirit'. The first hallelujah he made the foundation, calling it 'Zion'. In the second hallelujah he shewed forth how Moses carried out the work of the Tabernacle, and this he called a 'Song of the Heights'. And when they heard the sound of his voice, the king, the priests and the king's nobles ran to the church, and they spent the day in listening to him."

"So, you see," said Sister Sarah, "our music is designed for our churches. Every village has one. Prester John was so grateful for all God had given us in Amhara. God is the sole Creator in the universe, and we worship his glory together in a whole-hearted act of love, joy, music and celebration."

"Yes," said Imlac. "Devotion is an essential part of the spiritual practice taught by Prester John, to lead us to self-realization. It is the *sine qua non*, without which nothing will ever happen. Anyway, I shall take you to a church soon. This afternoon we have a further lecture in the Academy."

Sister Sarah went on, "We use rattles and goatskin drums. We also dance a great deal in the way King David, the great psalmist, the son of Solomon, the lover of our Queen of Sheba, danced and sang before his Lord, whom to us is God, consciousness, love or Self. It was King David who wrote in his forty-fifth psalm, 'Be still and know that I am God'.

"So this non-dual way must have been known to the Israelites in biblical times. But most of our music is vocal. We call it the Ethiopian chant. Christianity came here about 330 AD, brought by Fromentius. We have our own musical notation called *meleket*. It consists of characters from our ancient language *Ge'ez*. Each sign is a syllable and a cue for the melodic formula or *serayan*.

"The singer richly embellishes his singing with improvised melodic ornament. Some are cheerful and some are solemn. Here we train not only for musical accompaniment on stringed instruments, brass, woodwind, and percussion, but also we teach chanting, dancing and the composition of music, song, and liturgical poetry. We will ask Adam to demonstrate."

Adam, a tall young man, entered. He was accompanied by the drummer I had seen before, and another man with a rattle. Against this background of percussion, he began to chant while swaying sinuously in what seemed to be a mystic dance, his feet beating a regular rhythm and turning while he sang.

He reminded me of some of the dervishes I had seen in Konya in Turkey, the whirling Sufis of the great poet Jalludin Rumi. His voice rose and fell melodiously from bass to counter-tenor in a deeply moving way. It was astonishing to hear this range of vocal virtuosity. The chant was devotional and celebratory.

I could see that Tafara was as close to tears as I was. I felt that my whole being was being lifted out of its conventional little self, to an exaltation and an emotion of overwhelming thanksgiving to the Divine. I felt full of love for the whole of Creation, and gratitude for being alive.

Was this, I pondered, the objective music which Gurdjieff

talked about and brought back to the West from the Middle East in his sacred movements? This was a speculative thought, bringing me back to earth as Adam completed his chant. I do not think I have heard such beauty of sound, even from the great Italian operatic tenors.

Then Adam changed to a solemn chant. Immediately I felt impelled to fall on my knees and prostrate before the Holy of Holies, the One without a Second, the King and Ruler of the Universe, the microcosm of whom was in my heart, as I had just learned at the Academy. Again I started to weep, as did Tafara.

Imlac gazed at us compassionately. Seeing we were overwhelmed, he waited for Adam to finish and then simply said, "Come." We said our farewells to Sister Sarah and Adam. On the way back, Imlac promised that we could visit other colleges, and he would take us to a church tomorrow. Meanwhile, we must take a much-needed lunch and rest, to be ready for his next academy lecture.

We then walked back to the splendid golden dome of the Academy. When I had recovered, I asked Tafara to enlarge on the possibility that Amhara was the site of the Garden of Eden.

"Yes," said Tafara. "Don't you know the lines in *Genesis*: 'From the Garden of Eden flowed four rivers; the Tigris, the Euphrates, the Pishon and the Gihon. The Gihon, in three Septuagint texts, surrounds the land of Ethiopia. St. Bonaventura was convinced that Eden was here, and that Gihon was the Nile. We are near the Nile's source, as you know.

"Of course, some cite Mesopotamia as the site of Eden, but the great Magus Prester John was convinced that Amhara was Eden. That is why he chose this to be the center of his empire, and why such auspicious work for the benefit of humanity flows from this place."

Back in the sitting room we found a splendid buffet lunch laid out for us. After eating and drinking some delicious *teja* and soundly resting, we went to the lecture hall, a now-familiar sight, packed full of attentive, silent students.

Chapter 10

The Principles of Awakening

I will... bring you the length of Prester John's Foot
Benedick, in William Shakespeare's *Much Ado About Nothing*,
II.1.240

Imlac ascended the podium with great dignity. I could see his
gaze scan the audience. Little smiles of recognition flickered
around his lips as his eyes connected with each member of the
audience. A kind of transmission, I thought. When he looked at
me, I was certain of this, because I suddenly experienced a surge
of bliss issuing from the right side of my chest. Imlac had
invoked my Self, only if for a moment. But I had received a taste
and I knew its presence there.

"Today I am going to discuss the final principle. This is that
the awakening which is itself truth only happens when there is
immediate and direct perception or, better put, *apperception*. It
can only happen in the absence of reason and logic, which have
their roots in duality.

"In such understanding, the comprehender, 'the me', as an
individual entity, is totally absent. The mind is in an unconditional state of surrender. This awakening can spring only out of
absolute silence, the stillness that prevails when action ceases,
conflict ends and the ego is no more. Are there any questions?"

"Yes." At this point a beautiful young woman stood up and,
smiling gracefully, said, "Imlac, hello." Imlac nodded with a
warm smile. They exchanged gazes. "Tell me, is this understanding or awakening the same as enlightenment or self-
realization?"

"Yes, these are synonymous terms."

"Then what is their basis please?"

Imlac smiled. "First you must fully understand intellectually – this is the preliminary step, after much long practice of self-enquiry. You must recognize that every object, all phenomena that are perceivable in this manifestation we call Creation, are merely appearances in consciousness."

"I don't quite follow this."

"Very good. Would anyone please explain this point to Miriam?"

A young man stood up. His eyes were shining. I detected a radiance behind the swarthy, refined face of the Amharan.

"Yes, it is simple. We only see the surfaces of objects. Their colors are only the reflections of the light they cannot absorb. The substratum of these objects is also consciousness, which arranges the elements as it wills. All objects are in process or in a state of flux, including the human being.

"The whole affair is a magic picture-show projected on the retina, received by the brain and incorrectly interpreted. It is relative to man's sensory perceptual apparatus. The illusion is sustained by all humans as a species. It is really like a dream. My cat has a universe too, relative to its own sensory apparatus. In fact the reality, or thing-in-itself, of any object, cannot be known or seen by the eye. An electron microscope such as we have in the Science College gives us a clue, as does quantum physics: atoms and electrons are in a dance."

He paused for breath and continued. "On close examination, everything comes from no-thing, consciousness, and dissolves back into no-thing or consciousness. It is wonderful!"

"Good," said Imlac. "Please go on."

"Well, the senses are deceived by touch to think that objects are solid, whereas they are not at all – they contain a great deal of space. So the empirical world is merely an appearance in our own pure consciousness, a kind of screen on which the moving colored pictures come and go." He sat down.

"Does that help you, Miriam?"

Miriam got up and said that it had helped her and thanked them both for their explanation.

Imlac then continued. "These objects are perceived and cognized by consciousness itself, through the mechanism of dichotomy, or by splitting them up as an imaginary subject called 'me', and then an object, called 'he', 'she' or 'it'. Is that clear?"

There was silence. Imlac went on. "Furthermore, the consciousness we call our normal waking state, such as most of you are in now, is a stepped-down consciousness. It is a reflection or mirrorization caused by the ego's thick obscuration. It has to be removed by self-enquiry and surrender, gradually and gracefully, for you to experience the full power of absolute pure consciousness with all its treasures.

"These treasures are unconditional love, supreme intelligence, power of silence, knowledge or *gnosis*, and much more, that you will discover when you reach that stage. This is the process of waking up from life's dream. Any questions?"

Timidly I got up. "Yes, Imlac, I can see how I feel that I am a separate individual perceiving objects, but what has that got to do with my mind?"

Imlac looked at me for a moment with full attention. Suddenly I felt as if his eyes blazed with fire, that an energy was coming from them which somehow landed on the right side of my chest. Then I felt I was glowing. I didn't understand what was happening. Then he spoke.

"My dear traveler, explorer, visitor, and friend. You have a brain, a gift from God, like all your organs. This is a beautiful little mini-computer, much finer and subtler than any of the modern inventions which are mere products of the same brain. Every animal has one according to its needs and its place in the universal scheme.

"Have you ever pondered on the miracle of a fly's brain?

What is in that pin-head? Think about the mosquito, how its radar senses blood in the body of a human or animal, seeking its food. What a brain!" Some of the audience laughed.

"Now your eyes receive the sensory perception of an object, or you hear a sound or smell a smell, and so on. The brain, call it intellect, like a good western computer, opens a file triggered off by the object. These files are associative memories of all the impressions received about that object hitherto, and saved. With electronic speed, the brain makes comparisons, judgments, and discriminates or rejects. What a good tool for the empirical, relative world it is!

"But it is not for understanding the immanent and transcendent, all-pervading, all-sustaining consciousness-awareness, That which you really are. This mind must be surrendered to the Self, so it becomes a servant, not the master of your life. You have identified with your brain and its thought-patterns. You have labeled this hotchpotch of images 'me', an imaginary entity which doesn't really exist. A ghost, a phantom, a demon, responsible for all our anxiety, fear and grief. We have mistaken this rope of a world for a snake, as the ancient Rishis said."

"Ah," I said. "Thank you. I see better now. Please go on."

"So this process of brain reaction to perceived objects includes another thought-stream, which comes out of the blue, as it were. This is the process we call, for want of a better term, 'conceptualization' or thought. That's enough for today. We shall continue with this theme at our next lecture."

I was amazed at these people's ability to absorb these highly philosophic concepts, but Happy Valley could well be called the Land of Amazing Surprises. We returned to our rooms to relax, enjoy supper and a walk under the stars. We had some fine Amharic wine, a vintage, I mused, from the Garden of Eden.

Then I wondered if I dared try one of their apples – look what happened to Eve! She ate from the Tree of Knowledge, which I suppose was the conceptual thought Imlac was talking about. As

Tafara and I were together for the evening, I took advantage of the situation and asked him to tell me more about Sheba and Solomon's son, and what happened to him in Ethiopia.

Tafara answered by telling me, "There is a great deal recorded in the *Kebra Negast*, which means 'the Glory of the Kings'. This is an ancient book which gives the mythological history of Abyssinia, regarded as having scriptural authority in Ethiopia. There are several chapters about Solomon and Sheba, but I will tell you about their son, according to this record.

"First of all, she called her son by Solomon *Bayna-Lehkem*, which means 'Son of the Wise Man'. At twelve-years old he enquired who his father was. Although he was refused this information twice, on the third request the queen told him it was King Solomon, but that his kingdom was a very long way away. Apparently, as he grew up, he strongly resembled his father. Combined with the beauty of Sheba he was a most handsome youth.

"By the age of 22 he was a skilled hunter and warrior. He then announced to his mother that he intended to go to see his father and would return, by the will of God. The queen arranged for her chief minister and a rich merchant, named Tamrin, to prepare a caravan loaded with gifts, and to take the young prince to see Solomon and then bring him back. She would then make him king of Ethiopia in her place.

"He arrived at Gaza, a land which Solomon had already presented to Sheba. In the *Acts of the Apostles* you will find, in chapter 8, verse 27, that Luke tells the story of his meeting Phillip when he was baptized. It mentions him as a soul of great authority under Candace, another name for Sheba, who had visited Jerusalem. In Gaza the son was mistaken for Solomon himself, so great was the likeness. Word was sent to Solomon of his arrival.

"Solomon was glad because at that time, this was his only son except for Rehoboam, who was only seven years old. He sent many gifts to Bayna-Lekhem and sent soldiers to escort him. When Solomon saw him, he exclaimed, 'Behold, my father David hath renewed his youth and hath risen from the dead!'

Bayna-Lehkem, after rejoicing with his father, conveyed a message from his mother for Solomon, asking him to give a portion of the Tabernacle covering so it could be worshipped in her kingdom. But Solomon had other ideas: he wished his first-born to become king of Israel, staying in Jerusalem. But Bayna-Lekhem said he wished to stay in Ethiopia with his mother, asking again for a portion of the Tabernacle covering to take back.

"In spite of further attempts at persuasion, Solomon failed to make him remain. Bayna-Lekhem was, however, anointed by the priest Zadok, with Solomon's consent, and he was proclaimed Menelek I (from Bayna-Lehkem), king of Ethiopia, also to be called King David II. Then Solomon appointed 21 nobles to return with the new king to Ethiopia.

"The nobles were not too happy about having to leave their own country without the Tabernacle, and a plot developed to steal the Tabernacle of Zion from the Temple and take it with them to their new land for worship. Azariah, one of the nobles, and his three brothers, finding the Temple doors open, took the Tabernacle to Azariah's house and spread purple cloths over it to hide it.

"After being blessed by Solomon, David II left for Ethiopia with a caravan and the nobles, and with the Tabernacle hidden in a chariot. As they were leaving, Solomon told Zadok to give them the covering they had asked for on arrival. Then the party departed, and according to the *Kebra Negast* it was led by none other than the Archangel Michael, who spread out his wings to make the seas dry land.

"When they arrived back in Ethiopia there was very great rejoicing. The people saw that Ethiopia, like Israel, was to be a kingdom of God now that King David II had brought the Tabernacle with him from Jerusalem."

"What happened in Israel when they discovered the Tabernacle had gone?"

"Zadok nearly died with terror and Solomon summoned his army to pursue the Ethiopians. But he was too late, as they had already crossed the sea. Solomon lamented and saw it as the wrath of God, for the Israelites had practiced magic and materialism. But a spirit of prophecy consoled him and told him that what had happened had been God's will – and his first-born son was hardly an alien.

"It was believed to be deposited at Axum. But like your Holy Grail in England, it has been lost. All our priests carry representations of the Ark of the Covenant, or the Tabernacle, on their headpieces.

"It is getting late now and, another evening, I will continue with stories from the great and holy *Kebra Negast*. I hear your British Library has an English translation. James Bruce made a copy and gave it to the Bodleian. The British Museum received one from the Makdala Collection. Anyway, I believe that Imlac is taking us to see a church tomorrow."

We returned to our respective rooms and slept well, although I did dream a nightmare of a wrathful King Solomon pursuing his son and capturing him in Egypt. When I woke up I realized that it was just a dream, like the dream of life from which Amhara might awaken me. Or was Amhara also a dream?

Rather than confuse myself too much, I joined Tafara for the coffee ceremony and a light breakfast. Then Imlac arrived, looking splendid and radiant as ever.

"We are going to visit a church," he announced, with some fervor breaking through his otherwise sober voice.

As we walked, Imlac explained that each village had a church to house its 2,000 citizens. "These are built by the Masonic Guild on the principles of Solomon's Temple, proportionally designed around the number four in such a way as to create a sacred architecture evoking an atmosphere of awe and worship. The Knights

Templar had discovered the same laws when they excavated the ruins of Solomon's Temple in Jerusalem just before the Crusades, then to build Gothic marvels all over Europe.

"The churches are also used as assembly halls. Any important news or developments in the community or in other parts of Amhara can be announced there. People are also informed about significant events and trends in the outside world. We have no newspapers, radio or television like you do in the West – a salacious media which pollutes peoples minds, 'sowers of evil' as Gurdjieff used to call them."

I pondered on this. Newspapers are necessary in the West as a fourth estate to campaign against and curb corruption, misgovernment and injustice, but unfortunately they support false materialistic culture by promoting fashionable, glamorous lifestyles, playing upon people's fears to sell products and control society. Here in Amhara there was no such need.

Imlac seemed to read my train of thought. "But we have poetry and literary magazines, philosophical journals and personal news relating to deaths, births and happenings, recorded every week in an official gazette. But there are no journals in the way you have them. Sport here is played for the enjoyment of the games, not for running businesses."

I said to Imlac that I understood. But I could not understand why, if everything was perfect here and graduates were helping the world by their hidden influence, there were significant troubles in Ethiopia. It seemed a land ravaged by wars, violence, drought, famine and abject poverty.

"You need to understand something about cosmic balance," said Imlac. "It may be best understood by the concept 'where there is light there is also dark'. The whole of Creation is in perfect harmonious balance, but from a human perspective this cannot be understood. Prester John explained it something like this. The world is not centered on humanity. Without his invented ideals and motivations, the individual is terrified of being a nothing, in a purposeless, meaningless world. In fact, man's ideals of purpose are nothing but his own conditioned concepts.

"Nature cannot be seen or understood in terms of human thought, logic or language. What appears cruel and unjust on this planet seems so only when considered from the viewpoint of a separated, estranged individual. But nature is unconcerned because it is not human-hearted. Life is a field of destiny or karma, as the Rishis termed it.

"Every life is preordained for his or her spiritual development. There is no death. There is a cycle of continued rebirths until self-realization, when the world dream collapses and the soul reaches another plane of being or existence. 'You will find out when you get there', as Prester John used to say.

"But enough of this diversion. You have come to visit one of our churches. These are built out of the rocks, carved by the Mason's Guild using much of the knowledge that Solomon passed on to his beloved Sheba."

We came to a beautiful church. It was cut into a hill of rose-red stone, rather similar to those I had seen when I once explored Petra in Jordan. We entered an imposing porchway, cut into the west façade. It was magnificently carved, with what were obviously important scenes in Amharic history. The church was hollow, hewn from the rock, and the interior shape was as if a cross had been superimposed onto a pentagram.

The walls were decorated by magnificent brightly-colored frescoes, showing scenes of the lives of Solomon, Sheba, Jesus and the towering figure of Emperor Prester John. The interior was supported by eight carved columns. At the head of the cross there was a carved stone altar. Large arched windows had been carved into the outside rock, letting in volumes of light. The whole effect was one of profoundly awe-inspiring silence.

The atmosphere in this church also created a strong devotional atmosphere of obeisance to the divine force governing the universe. The reduction of the individual in relation to the scale of this divine power could be sensed. The feeling of separation from all that is seen and heard felt diminished. The air was perfumed by frankincense and myrrh, the sacred herbs that the Magi had brought to the infant Jesus.

The strong light filling the building mirrored an inner light which I felt filling the cave of my heart, which this church carved from solid rock seemed to symbolize. The building was domed in the Byzantine style. The dome was painted azure blue, dotted with encrusted gold reproductions of the constellations mirroring the heavens, at the same time containing the silence.

As I was musing on the overpowering wonder of this church, a congregation started to enter. Although draped in the traditional white cloaks, turbans for men and burkas for women, the men and women wore different colored turbans. Their waist sashes and scarves were also different-colored, matching the turbans and burkas. I asked Imlac to explain this and he told me that it indicated the guild or university college they were attending or had attended.

"We shall witness the Eucharist," said Imlac. A priest entered, wearing an embroidered red and gold fez-type hat. He wore a solid gold cross around his neck.

"The service will be in English, for your benefit," said Imlac. "I told them we had an English guest."

The priest started to chant in the same melodious manner of joyous celebration that I had heard in the Traditional Music School. I asked Imlac for a copy of the words after the service. It went as follows.

"Before the world was, and unto everlasting is God in His Kingdom, God in His triune nature, God in His divinity. Before the morning and the evening, and before the day and night, before the angels were created, was God in His Kingdom. Before the Heavens were stretched forth, and before the face of the dry land appeared, before the green herbs grew, was God in His

Kingdom. Before the sun and the moon and the stars, and before the orbits of the lights, was God in His Kingdom. Before the beasts that move and the birds that fly, before the creatures of the sea, was God in His Kingdom.

"Before He created Adam in His own image and likeness, and before man transgressed the commandment, was God in His Kingdom. Glory be to the Father and the Son and the Holy Spirit, now and ever, world without end. The priest sayeth: 'Holy, Holy, Holy, is God in His Trinity'. Though He was King, He showed His humility as a servant. He stretched forth His hands to the Passion – even He who had formed man – that He might free man from the yoke of ignorance.

"In that night in which He was betrayed, He took bread in His holy and blessed hands, which were without blemish. He looked up to heaven to Thee, His Father. He gave thanks, blessed and brake bread, and gave to His holy disciples and pure apostles, and said unto them, 'Take, eat. This bread is My body, which is broken for you for the forgiveness of your ignorance.' And again, He mingled water and wine. He gave thanks, blessed and hallowed, and delivered to His holy disciples and pure apostles, and said unto them, 'Take. Drink. This cup is My Blood, which is poured out for you, for a ransom for many.'

He died, who dieth not. He died to destroy death. He died to give life to the dead, even as He had promised them by the word of a covenant. They took Him down from the tree and wrapped Him in linen clothes, and buried Him in a new tomb. On the third day He rose from the dead, came to the place where His disciples were, and appeared to them in the upper room of Zion. And on the fortieth day, when He ascended to Heaven, He commanded them, saying, 'Wait for the promise of thy Father.' On the fiftieth day He sent His Holy Spirit in tongues, as of fire, and they spake together in the speech of all lands."

I felt I was in a sacred place of true devotion. It reminded me a little of the charismatic fervor of some our Christian Gospel churches in England, but this devotion went even deeper and was more profound.

The silver communion cup was passed and many swayed in adoration of their beloved King of the Universe, God, Jesus, Love, Source, Heart, Brahman, Shiva, Buddha, Elohim, Allah. These names all meant the same to them. Tafara whispered that they chose the names to chant where they resonated the strongest. I felt that I was lifted to a transcendental, ecstatic place where there was no 'me', no sense of personal identity separating my self from all I was witnessing. I was one with everybody there. They were living in my spaciousness. They were all gods. I felt like a god too, and that all was love and in love, and that love was all that there truly was. When we left the Church of St. Thomas, I reported my experiences to Imlac.

"Yes," he said, "this is grace indeed. You have been given another free gift. But when you talked to me about it and expressed it in words, did you notice you dropped to the ordinary mental level again?"

I dropped back. It felt like falling down from a transcendental state to the ordinary level of mind-chatter and intellectualism.

"Well, you are definitely on the way. Who knows? Be careful, you may even wake up before you leave here!"

As we left the church we passed the village markets. They were open air affairs. Stall upon stall was laden with every kind of fruit, vegetable and craft utensil. It was a magnificent, colorful sight. I asked how they bought what they needed.

Imlac looked somewhat shocked. "Bought? Heavens forbid, no! As money and the personal accumulation of goods is the basis of the kind of competitively-driven society which makes slaves of its peoples and destroys their spiritual flowering, we would never permit such an idea. Didn't the great magus Moses warn against the worship of the golden calf, in no uncertain terms? Haven't his chosen people disobeyed his command ever since, paying a very heavy price for deserting their role as a holy people? Only their Hassidim seem to realize this. This money-based society destroys the natural loving relationship between fellow children of God. Here, people are free to have what they need."

"But suppose someone abuses this and starts to accumulate objects for their own sake and becomes greedy?"

"This is very rare, almost nonexistent. But in case someone abuses the trust, you are asked to sign a book for whatever you have taken. A quick perusal would point to such a sickness and an elder would discuss the matter with him or her. But I cannot remember a case in recent times."

"I believe this is the system the Israeli kibbutzim first used, before they became materialistic. They found it worked very well too. So you don't have courts of law either?"

"Good heavens, no! We have the Consultative Tribunal. As there is no private property, no accumulation of wealth and no money, we have no need for that accursed tribe of lawyers, accountants and bankers."

I laughed. This was utopia indeed. Sir Thomas More and all those writers whose imaginary states did without private property would be overjoyed at Amhara.

"What about the Classical Musical College?" I asked, to change the topic.

Imlac replied that it was run like our own academies of music in the West. I then asked him about drama schools. He replied to the affirmative, adding that real theatre is a very large part of Amhara's social life. He offered to take us to see a Mystery Play called *The Ark of the Covenant*. He ended the walk by saying that he had to leave us, as he was due to give an Academy lecture after lunch, and he had to prepare.

After wining, resting and dining, we went to the packed lecture hall. Imlac was at the lectern and began.

"Such understanding as we have digested up to now leads to the direct apperception of the true nature of the human being. It is then perfectly clear that the phenomenal manifestation, the basis of sensory illusion, is not representative of the process of life as simply birth, then life, then death and rebirth, until realization takes place."

"Imlac, I have a question."

"Yes, Azariah." Imlac seemed to know the names of his students.

"How is it the basic illusion?"

"Well, study one of our favored Abyssinian cats. He has his own world, universe even. Consciousness animates him, the same consciousness that animates us all, and his tiny brain interprets what his senses contact, as does every insect, animal and sentient being, including man and woman. All creatures, although animated by the one absolute pure consciousness which is God, are limited by the spectral range of their senses and the discriminating possibilities of their computing brains. So this is why I say it is the basic illusion."

"Thank you, Imlac. Please proceed."

"It is then abundantly clear that the basic illusion is a mistaken belief in an objective entity called Azariah, or Zadok the cat, for example – the so-called 'me'. Of course, Zadok the cat barely self-references to his identity as we do. Our 'me' is composed of a bundle of thoughts, an intricate network of conditioned reactions to any given situation or set of circumstances in which it finds itself placed by its predetermined destiny. These patterns are sustained by memory. Look inside. Close your eyes, try hard, with all your attention and concentration, to find anything substantial that even slightly resembles an entity or 'me'."

I noticed that most of the students closed their eyes. Imlac paused for a few minutes while this enquiry was carried out in silence.

"So, you see, anyone who has found a 'me' or any entity inside, please stand up."

No one replied.

"Good. This so-called 'me' is a fictional notion, a convenience to label your mind-body system with. Every we time we say 'me', it is a half-truth or half-lie. This I did, this happened to me, I did that, he touched me, and so on. This inaccuracy of language compounds an error. In truth, this happened, that happened, owing to an inevitable set of subtle and gross circumstances that the universe sets up every moment. This is God's will.

"The Source is the One Doer, and it does everything else, including man, who reacts according to the same divine will. But arrogant man ascribes his actions by habit to something he calls his free will. This illusory 'me' or 'I' appears to make choices, but that appearance is part of the structure of what is determined to happen. So man is hypnotized.

"Do you all understand this clearly? It is most important."

Something impelled me to say that this concept went against years of conditioning which would be difficult to break down.

"Ah," said Imlac. "I will give you an exercise to help. Over the next few days, at the end of each day, reflect on three or four of the most significant events which happen to you. Then enquire as to what extent your personal so-called will actually created these events and made them happen. If you are honest, you will realize that everything happens exactly in the way it only can, and the way the whole universe, from atom to galaxy, conspires to make it happen. That is God's will."

"Thank you," I said. "I will try."

"But", said Imlac, "Although the false sense of 'me' is an illusion, self-enquiry is essential to probe deeply and discover the root of that false sense of egotism or personal sense of doership. Dive deep, plunge into your heart through the ever open door on the chest's right side, and see if you can find it."

"At first this is done with the mind, so you will find nothing there at the bottom of the abyss. But persevere, and one day you will find the enquiry will start in the heart, triggered by emotional moments. This is the beginning of the ego's death. So persevere with determination, no matter how long it takes. If anyone needs personal guidance, make an appointment to see me or one other of our Tribunal members, who have awakened from the sleep of life. Now let's enjoy some deep silence for half an hour before we depart."

I looked forward to seeing the rest of the university – the medical, astrological and architectural schools, the Painters' Guild, and much more. A hospice where the dying are helped to completely surrender to the Divine Will, and stay thinking of the Godhead. This practice could lead them to Enlightenment, and they would not have to endure another rebirth on this dark planet.

But the next morning I was in for a very great surprise! Imlac came to see me, looking very serious and grave.

"Justin, the members of the Supreme Tribunal have just decided, after deep astrological consultation, that this is precisely the exact time the harassed outside world should know something about us. Tafara, because he is a native of Ethiopia, is to stay with us and complete his education in the Academy, to reach, eventually, Self-Realization.

"But we insist that you, dear Justin, return and write some account of your experiences, and what you have discovered here. It is very important that the knowledge of Amhara's existence, its teaching and its society, reaches the outside world. This is a critical time in the planet's evolution, when there is confusion and disorder everywhere, spiritually, economically and morally. It is of the uttermost importance that you go and do this for us, and humanity's sake!" His voice rose in intensity and his manner was most imperative. I could not dare to object, such was his demeanor. "You will be taken from here tomorrow, safely back to Addis Ababa, to board a flight home. There is to be no discussion about this. Our minds are firmly made up!"

"Of course, neither you nor the people who read your book,

which you must write as soon as possible, will ever be able to find their way to enter Amhara. That will be strictly reserved for advanced mature souls who are ripe for our esoteric knowledge. We shall know who and when they will come, as we knew that you and Tafara were coming. But, don't worry, we will put you in touch with one of our Enlightened Messengers, secretly to be hidden, but to live near where you live. We shall send him into the world to help you when your book is finished. You shall be informed. He will lead you to Enlightenment, have no fears or doubts in this respect. Sincere people who read your book will also find help if they really earnestly and sincerely wish for it, as time moves on, after all this is the Age of Aquarius, the water bearer of Truth!"

I was deeply shocked and saddened to think that I must now leave the wondrous Happy Valley. But I understood and accepted the fact that these wise and intelligent people must have very good reasons for my dismissal. As I was told and remembered, Prester John had said that "everything happens for the best, in the best of all possible worlds, even if we never understand the Higher Wisdom at the time. There is no death. If we think something is bad, it is only because we don't under-stand it." I was satisfied, however, that I had discovered a great deal about the profound truths that they taught and the wonderful way that these beautiful people organized their society. I now had a very worthwhile mission to perform as soon as possible, and to tell the world about some of the wonders of Amhara that I had been shown!

On the way back in the Ethiopian Airways jet, I had a sudden revelation. I fell into a deep trance that seem to envelop my whole mind and body. It was an intuitive recognition that the marvelous people of Amhara had discovered a tremendous secret for humanity, a new way of being. Furthermore, the seed which I would plant would grow into a huge tree and our planet could move forward to happier, more fulfilling days, when we would witness a great step forwards toward an evolved humanity, as the Higher Powers had always intended. Then, I dozed off, and the next thing I knew was that I had landed back at my London airport, once more into the harassed dream world of life as we know it. The more placid, real world of Amhara was now only a memory, but one which would stay with me for the rest of my days.

B O O K S

O is a symbol of the world, of oneness and unity. In different cultures it also means the "eye," symbolizing knowledge and insight. We aim to publish books that are accessible, constructive and that challenge accepted opinion, both that of academia and the "moral majority."

Our books are available in all good English language bookstores worldwide. If you don't see the book on the shelves ask the bookstore to order it for you, quoting the ISBN number and title. Alternatively you can order online (all major online retail sites carry our titles) or contact the distributor in the relevant country, listed on the copyright page.

See our website **www.o-books.net** for a full list of over 500 titles, growing by 100 a year.

And tune in to myspiritradio.com for our book review radio show, hosted by June-Elleni Laine, where you can listen to the authors discussing their books.

mySpiritRadio